LOOKING OUT MY PROJECT'S WINDOW

JAY MONROE

Looking Out My Project Window.

40BEES ENTERTAINMENT, INC
40-15 30TH AVENUE BOX 118
ASTORIA, NEW YORK 11103

ISBN: 978-0-9816668-0-8

Library of Congress Cat. Num. in-Pub.-Data

PRINTED IN THE UNITED STATES OF AMERICA

40 Bees Publishing Presents: Looking out my projects window

Cover Design by Nohjcoley

Rest in Peace

Alberta Mae Brown

Sunrise
Sunset
January 14, 1921
December 11, 2007

Acknowledgement

I would like to thank God, for giving me the strength to keep going when mostly everyone around me was in doubt. Expect for a chosen few that are with me no matter what battle or crisis I was in. My moms, my wife Raquel, my lil girls Johnesha and Jalisse. Kora, Zinga, my nephew and nieces. My bro Ygee and Worm hold your head. Nancy, Bgee, Lisa, Jonelle and Storm, Val, Lisa, Tc, Sartara, Muffy, Nayvon the Chisholm Family, Gidget, Lee-Lee, Poppy, Eric, Angie, Courtney, Jap, Reese, Big homey Lord, Lisa and his family.. Tylon, Wells, Flip, Rap, lil Bee, Buddha, JL, Smooth, IU, AD, Whip, Bump, Jay Rock, Fredo, Big Chick, BobRiis, Puba, Opps, lil black, Step, Slick, L, Paula, Bam, Rambo, Shaheem,12, Zaza, Miss Georgia, Marcell, Mike Chapfield, C-Wop, Fonz, Darren, Malik, Kas, The Alston Family. LES, Dave& Terry, Mr. Russell, Petey Greene, Sonny, Slim, Mr. Kenny Dude, Andrew, Pop, Mr.Tee, Kenya Bland, My homey for life Mary, the dime block, Draws, Miss Ruby. Monica, Black Robby, Kevia, Meika, Lake, Super, Rob, Bullet, big bee, lil bee , Crazy Cliff Ty-sleee, Rondu, Keke, Cedric, Jah west, Edee, Junior, Jason, The Twins, Nascell, Quanell, Daweed, Green Eyes, Felton, Todd, Janay, Brother Dean, Biz, Arkim, Hot Day, Trent, The Franklin Family, Ray L, bodygee, Ruck, Carl & Brian Brody, the design work from my man nonjcoley, causal, Freeze, Teik, Ever, Joe, Deli, D-gotti, Denise, Nate, Kayron, Rocky, G-man, JP, Tom, Sal, Cliff, Joey, Anthony, GQ Lounge, Awax, Ravenswood Pj's, Hype North Carolina, Dezo, Smack, Head, Big Gary and Zane, Vic, Monty,Ju-Ju, Black Jason ATL, T-Day, Miss Mary, Sha-Sha, Gary, Tim& Pop Banks, Mo Dixon, Jerry, Greg, Mike Heron, Joel Ortiz, Axe, Rob, Flavor in ya ear and Hydra studios, Evil, George Urban Latino Mag. Steve Allhiphop.com, Anna, Gene, Gina, Macho. My dudes strength and Honor to Bang, Prinz, Wiz, Biglow, Burner, Boogie, Larry, 88,Sho, Pernell, Nish, Gutter, Needles, Black Shawn, Frankie Spires, Young, Nyquil, Hit, Shamel the CCF fam.

Ebony, Jessica, Lisa, Isaac, Momma, Boo-Gotti, Ock, Al Womack and family, Fendi, karate Joe, Bill, Johnnie, Skins, Germ, Face, Say, Q, Lucas, GOV, Twin, Nitti, Shamel, Nando, Just, OG, Woodside pj's Sheity and big homey, Grafh, Ock, Green eye Un, Blackhand, Judu, Maino, Eight o, Blackflag Hustle Hard, C-Bee, Moo-Moo, Fort Greene, Uncle Murda, East New York, Tee, Tree, Eddie, Cash, Felon mag, Dam, Ike, Suave, Phil, House, CJ, Ski, L, Missy, Terri, Miss Smith, Robin, Tweet, Tonya, Aunt Bee, Curtis, Denise, Lucky ,Frankie , Larry, EB, Donnell, Nard, Su, Morris, Snacks, Calvin, Sloopy, Drac .Candy, Nay-Nay, Mecca, Kathy, Laurel, Pat , Hiwill, RobFace, Maurice, Peace, Tommy God, Boog, Drano, Dip, Mo Money, Lil Black, Tray Bag, Poppy Star, Born, Just, Penny, Nellie, Toya, Puzzle, Miss Motty, Jamel, Tiny, Cisco, Lee, My Godmother Yolanda New Platz N.Y. Miss Barbara, Aiesha, Puff, Pudding, Roshawn, Nolia, Sherron, Nicole Talley, Baby sham, Surge, Moon, Laurel, Melba, Naydean, Meika, Kevia, Miss Mary, Tenia, Shante, Genie, Macho, Nino, Tameha, Fucky Child, Monique Hines, Mousey, Monifa, Slim, Losha, Cash, just, Preme, CIB Far rock, 1main, Tee-Tee, Donna, Nookie, Claria, Trina, Gary, Jamel, Miss Dee, Inf& Sha keep filming them dvds Hostagemusik, Tiger, H, Cee-Gutter, Redhook pj's the Lefrak Fam Rah, Carlos, Rob, Sha, Judah, Dirt, Baggy Nore, Rell Snoop, Shameek ,Trevor Bailey, DayQuil, Tanisha, Sweat,Yatti, ,Raborn, True, Powerful ,Keith, Tweet, Charlie Brown, Corley Wall, Mook ,Ki, Hit 'em up Ent. , Rondu, Slab, Sonny Black, Huff, 40 pj's Mike Kidd, coach Bill Bano, Kevin the Portland trailblazers, Ron Artest, Jose, Sincere, Man-child Mariam's Soul food. Delsun, Don Diva mag, Dr Bob Lee WBLS All of the QB rappers that are doing it Nas, Marley marl, Shan, Roxanne Shante, Mobbdeep, Cormega, Alchemist, Mega, Capone, Nature, Craig Gee, ACD, BARS&Hooks, Blitz, Littles, Poet, Dimples Dee, Crime Family, Infamous mob, Big Twin and Godfather, Grand Wiz, Jungle, Nashawn, Nazarine, Chicky, Iman Thug,

Tragedy, Noyd and All THE OTHERS!!. Music, Green, CK keep rolling them dice them buddy Donte, Bee, Kastro, Crisis, Buddy, Kdot, Peso, Lord Black, Shady, Snakes, Tyheim, Freedom, Knowledge, Woody, Mark Pringle, Ra, John, Life, Felicia, Rick, Weasel, E.Rhodes Freaky TY, Jamean, Nicole, AC Astoria pj's Pam, Helen, Vanessa, Michele, Tara, Tilly, Miss Linda, Miss Sharon, Butter, Corrine, Ms. Freedom, Ebony, Keri, Gloria, Mecca, Tammy, Illyana, Poohie, Kima, Boo-Boo and her family Tamara, Left, John, Main, Ruck, Messiah, Amar, Watts, Slick, Miss Watson, Kecia, Preme, Kecia's soul food Ricardo Bentham, Phoenix Services, Rev. Taylor the center of hope, Starr, Cassidy ,Young, Unique, Stacey, Miss Linda, Bigger Utcia ave, Jaesupreme, Gary, Party Rob, 80, Tanieka, Tonya, Momma, marine Terrance, Vic Coles, Big Face Productions, Dante " The hood" Ebandte Inc. Publishing, Miz, Pen Cushion Publishing, Shaborn Dewey Hill Publishing. Teri Woods, Kwan GANSTA Good lookin Brother, Big Storm, Perkect Storm, Vox Music Group, Smack, Shea Davis, Smack DVD, Frenchie, Cocaine City, Sub zero. The north and south side of QB. It is so many people I will doing this all day. Just bless y'all all and much success to anything you do. If I didn't acknowledge you my bad love is love. Also to Linda for giving me this chance and isn't nothing but good things follow!! To all my comrades locked down hold your head and keep fighting hit them laws books and find that loophole.   Peace and love

Chapter 1

Queensbridge projects are one of the biggest housing developments in the city of New York. It has 96 buildings, six floors and six apartments on each floor in every building. It is right next to the 59th street bridge, if you took the upper level you could see it, and from that high up it looked like a maze, a sprawling 49acres housing project with its poverty-stricken community.

Sometimes it reminds him of a small town down South. All of the older people in the south on nice days gather on their porches and then on Sunday mornings go to church. These be the same hypocritical people that be talking about everyone that passes them by.

The only differences between the south and the projects is here they sit on benches or build at card tables, and instead of talking on their porches they do it while playing cards. In between every hand they stop and talk about all of the people that walk by. Passing judgment on everyone like they're the most righteous people that walked on this earth.

Since he lived on the first floor, outside his window were these benches, sometimes Carlos just listened to them talk.

A few times he heard them talk about his family, but he would just laugh it off. However one day they sat on that bench talking about his family and it made him upset. See there was this older white haired lady named Miss Johnson and Miss Johnson had a great deal of hate towards his family. He would never forget the day that he was listening and he heard her say," Isabelle's youngest son and his friends are out there selling drugs, the middle boy been in and out of jail since he was 12, and don't forget about her daughter that got life in jail. Carlos's older sister Valerie stabbed two girls to death in a drug- induced rage five years ago. ' Miss Jackson, Carlos' next door neighbor stopped her before she could continue, she said," Miss Johnson what to you expect, that family doesn't have any positive role models to look up to."

Carlos backed away from the window, her words hit a nerve in him. He was Isabelle's youngest son, he wanted to go slap Miss Johnson from here to next month. Carlos grabbed his jacket he needs to get away from what he was hearing. As he was about to walk out the door, his mother notices the look of disappear on his face. She knew Carlos very well especially when he was angry, she wanted to know what was wrong. He told her what Miss Johnson had said, she ordered him to sit and calm down.

His mother was all they had and she could throw some jewels at them that would calm them down and make them think, she said," Carlos if you was to get mad at everything someone says, you would be out there fighting all the time, and that would eventually lead to prison, boy you cant pay those ignorant women that sit on those benches no dam mind. If their asses worried abut their own kids as much as they worry about everyone else's maybe her 14 year old grandbaby wouldn't be having a baby. Don't pay them no mind them old bitties don't do nothing for our family." He seen it in his mother's eyes, the pain and hurt because words do sting, especially when it's the truth. Isabelle was real she only spoke the truth to her kids. The pain she was feeling was because she knew that anyone of her kids could end up in a 12 by 12 cell for the rest of their lives living in the projects. That was the reality for the life of her kids and it saddens her deeply.

No one wants that for their children, but a single mother raising seven kids on her own in the projects, Isabelle knew that was one of the many daily challenges her children faced. She knew her kids weren't angels, shit far from it but they were hers and all she could do is pray they find a path out of the projects.

Some of the mother's in the hood live in their own world where they think their kids can do no wrong, but the truth is that they're doing everything wrong under the sun, selling drugs, prostituting, taking drugs, stealing, we all know what goes on in the projects.

Well Miss Johnson's statement hit home it made Carlos take a deep look at not only his life but the lives of his sisters and brothers, but yet in all he knew that deep down in his heart that his mother did her best to raise her kids the right way. They just chose the wrong paths, you got to realize in a place like this all you see growing up was murder, drug selling, robbery, number running, credit card scams, you name it, it was done here. Once Carlos seen this lady walking around asking people for money to lay her 5 year old son to rest properly, he later found out she was lying, she just wanted the money to buy drugs.

There was auto pistols on the streets and crack was a powerful force, as soon as you exit the elevator and walk down the stairs you could smell crack in the hallways, it wasn't hidden, it wasn't a dark or bad thing, It was all out in the open. This was an everyday occurrence so you get used to it smelling that odor everyday. The thing that bothered him the most was, Miss Johnson, who was Miss Johnson to judge anyone, it's oblivious she made a few wrong decisions in her life to be sitting, talking about people on the bench at 69 years old in the projects.

In the projects it is like you're living in a box and there are people all around you. Everyone's going though some kind of struggle, because you wouldn't be living here if you weren't. You have to deal with the stress of everybody's struggle every single day. Don't get me wrong the projects are where you develop your creativity. If you are not fortunate to have a jump rope you get a clothing line and make one. You come up with games to keep you and your friends happy. It's not jail, we have fun, kids playing skeely and other games we could make up along with playing basketball, which was our favorite past time. However living in the projects everyday was filled with tension, and that is similar to jail. You had to be smart and navigate your way though it. Not to say all negative things come out of places like this, but all those who live here are challenged.

Marley Marl, Mc Shan, Nas, Mobb Deep, Cormega, Nature, Screwball, Lake, Littles and a few up and coming rappers come from here. Both of the Fleming brothers went to the NBA, one to the Pacers and other to the Celtics. Ron Artest just made it to the Bulls. Lou Del Valle is a boxer, he fought Roy Jones for the title. His friend Maurice is a top executive at Arista, this huge record label. Not only does the place create athletes and music artist, but a few became lawyers, cops and schoolteachers. Most of the people who live here want to make it out, but not everyone will. Like all projects you have the ones that never leave their block! Some are content with not working or working for welfare.

The broken down school system where you have to enroll your children in hopes of them getting an education. Teachers who only work for a paycheck, along with waiting for the school bell to ring like the kids, potentials lost and shit like that. A lot of people fell victim to the ghetto demands drugs and hustling just to name a few.

Its bad enough we're born in an environment like this, but wanting to stay here is crazy. Carlos believed that when you're born in the jungle, it's hard to adapt to change, but just like the wild, you have to prepare because you know things are only going to get wilder, after all in the jungle there is no right or wrong.

Carlos was born in New York hospital to his loving mother Isabelle. Carlos was her fifth child, his mother was Spanish 5'1, 140 pounds. She moved to Queensbridge from Brooklyn a few years before he was born. His father Charles was a New York City Police Officer, Carlos was named after his mother's brother, Carlos. According to his moms and pops he favored his uncle and his mother always told him that. His father wanted his mother to move down south to Greensboro N.C. with him, but all she knew was the city life, so she stayed here to make a life for them.

His pops left them, he went down south to become a sheriff. He wouldn't see his dad again until he was 15 years old, and that meeting only took place, because of his Aunt Shirley. However them meeting again was a good one, he got to meet his half sister Kim, who he would see occasionally in Queensbridge, but didn't know she was family. Her grandmother lived in the hood, but Kim lived in Lefrak City.

His father asked him to move in with him, how in the hell was he going to move in with a stranger, he didn't know this man, so he refused. Three years later his father died in a car accident that was difficult for him so many mixed emotions but I knew it was time to forgive him for just abandoning them all, and forcing his mother to raise them alone. Carlos vowed to never be like that to his children when he had his own.

That was the most valuable thing he learned from his dad. He believe that for your kids you have to make many challenging sacrifices, but you have to always keep in mind that the trails and tribulation children face growing up is hard for them. Here you have his mother by herself no job and five kids living in the projects.

Then finally a man that was willing to be there for his mother and her children entered our lives his name was Bill.

Bill was a butcher at the local meat market, that's where they met, they started going out a few months later, and then they got married. They had two baby girls his beautiful sisters, he also had three kids of his own from his last marriage. Stephanie, Donna, and Nelly all of them are older than him.

Bill jumped right in as a step dad. Bill's love for Carlos and his brothers and sisters was unique. However he always tried to encourage Carlos to be open-minded and look at a situation both ways. He wanted to teach him how to make better decisions in life and to be able to guide him to do the right things, but when you're young you don't realize how the decisions you make now, will later impact your life later.

Carlos was into them streets hard, doing armed robberies, breaking into stores and shit with Poppy and other dudes from the hood. Carlos quit school by the 10th grade, he always did well in school, but he was always fighting and stealing.

He remembered one time when he was in the 8th grade he was fighting some guys right next to the principle's office. The principle came out to stop the fight when Big Richie went crazy, he started throwing anybody that touched him, all you saw was fist flying so when the Principle grabbed him he went for the kill and broke that his nose. The school security officers held everyone down until the cops came. That was my first trip to juvenile hall, my mother and Bill came to get me.

Everyone got out except Richie, his mother was a crack fiend, she told," The cops they could keep his no good ass."

Carlos will always respect Rich, because when they went to court for that case Richie told the judge," fuck you, nobody did shit but me."

The court officers took him to the back, because of what Rich said, they let everybody else walk, but because of what went down none of us was wanted by any of the schools in district 30, but it's the law for us to get an education so they had to find schools that would take us, but of course they weren't going to keep all us to be together. Richie got sentenced to 3 to 5 years for the assault and for a gun case he had.

The board of education sent us all to different 600 schools, Carlos went to Sterling High. That's an all boys' school, just like jail. People taking people's lunch, sneakers, coats and tokens. That was the funny shit about the school, they would give us tokens, just like money, no train or bus passes. You had to wait until three to get your token to go home, so you could imagine how shit was after school.

At Sterling we were allowed to go outside for lunch, that shit was a joke, or should I say the few that had money and the funny shit was that if we found out you had money your knew your ass was getting jacked for it. McDonald's and Wendy's were right next to the school.

One day Carlos seen this kid get his ear cut off, because he wouldn't gave up his Big Mac. Both kids where in his school, one in his class, and the other on the next floor.

Most of the dudes he met there, unfortunately he would meet up with again on Rikers Island.

Rikers Island was the nation's largest jail a remote complex that sits in the east river in sight of LaGuardia airport or the juvenile center Spoftford. Here they house all kinds of criminals and for every crime possible. The levels of crimes ranged from one dude who shot a cop, to another for stealing a cop's horse in Central Park. He quit school after going there a year, he got to meet a few good dudes in there.

One of his mans was this dude he will never forget his name is Akbar, Carlos and him had a lot in common and they would sit and talk about taking over the drug game, he was a young hustler with the same ambition as him. He got murdered at the age of 17, over a girl.

The youngest guy he remembers getting killed was Tee, he got killed over some drugs in Maryland. His family moved there to get away from all the bad shit that was happening in New York City. Like the Geto Boys said," the world is a ghetto." The same problems that exist here exist in every poor neighborhood, sometimes 10 times worse. You can't run from the problems, it's up to you to find a solution.

Chapter 2

Carlos made it home in time for the summer. Shit the summertime in Queensbridge was crazy. Well shit was popping and Carlos was chilling. Money was tight and he was running up to Steinway to get right for the jam that was supposed to take place later that night. Girls, girls everywhere, the jam in the River Park was drawing people from all over. Grills were going everywhere, you could smell the mixture of chicken, steaks and BBQ two blocks away. All of the girls were dressed in Coke-Cola shirts, Benetton jeans, all of the hottest fashions of the year. Eric B and Rakim's "Eric B for president" was blasting from the speakers. Everyone was dancing having a good time.

Isabelle Carlos's mother, Miss Brenda and Miss Ford were cooking out in the park too, but they were located away from the jam.

Me, Shakim, and L walked over to where they were cooking to get something to eat. L was an average sized dude, with curly hair, a pretty boy. All L did was smoke weed, dress fly and mess with mad girls. He was more fortunate then the rest of us. His mother was an accountant at this law firm and his father was a union rep for the Phone Company. They moved out the projects a few years ago, now they live in a condo on 70th street in Manhattan.

Carlos remembers when him and his father had a big fight, because L was always in the streets. His father told him," If you're going to live here, you follow my rules or get out." L left, moved in with his aunt and two girl cousins. I could never understood L's ways, but he knew that feeling you get when you're getting fast money, you get hooked just like the fiends you sold to.

Carlos's mother made them all plates with Macaroni and cheese, rice and beans, corn, chicken, shrimps, and steaks. Isabelle asked Shakim, "How's your grandmother doing? I haven't seen her in a while, please tell her I said hello don't forget." Shakim said," she's doing fine, she's just so busy working both of her jobs, I'll make sure I tell her to call u." Isabelle said," Okay, make sure u tell her that, u staying out of trouble?" Shakim," yes, just trying hard to finish this computer school I'm in."

Carlos's Mother," keep at it you'll finish.

That's great you're doing something positive with yourself."

She was looking right at Carlos, he knew it was time to go before she started the lecture with him. Carlos walked over and kissed her on the cheek, then said," I love you, I want y'all to leave the park before it gets too dark." She said," we're adults, we'll leave when we're ready." Carlos looked at her and said," Mommy I just don't want nothing to happen, U know at these jams stuff gets crazy, when it gets dark."

She said," I know Carlos, we planned on leaving soon anyway." he said," Alright, y'all got help packing this stuff up?" She said," yeah, Brenda's sons are on their way down here." Carlos said," okay and bye to Miss Ford and Brenda.

They all waved to one another, then they walked off. Shakim, that's my main man. He's a little on the heavy side, but that was cool, the ladies were still sweating him.

Shakim was always on the right track, he just hung out with them, because they all grew up together on the same block. Shakim's dream was to work at a computer programming company. He went to school everyday, no matter how late they hung out. He lived with his grandmother, his moms just left him to move with some guy in the Bronx. That's about a 20-minute train ride from here, but he never went to see her, nor did she come to see him.

Shakim, L, and me started talking. Shakim said," yo, did y'all see that girl Tomeika from Vernon?" L said," yeah, I seen her! She's a hoe, all them niggas from Astoria be fucking her and once she gets back to the hood, she thinks she's miss high-class." Carlos said," Word, that bitch is crazy, got four kids, all by different fathers, at 18." Shakim said," I don't care, I just want to bone her at least once." They all laughed.

The jam was banging, everybody was dancing, having a good time. The deejay put on Mc Shan's hit the bridge, the whole park started too wild out. Shakim went and got on this girl's backside, L and Carlos did the same thing.

They danced a few more records, drank a few 40 ounces of Olde English and talked. DS, Chip, Tank and Carlos's brother just got there. They walked over, they all slapped each other's outstretched palms and started vibing. DS pulled Carlos's to the side, away from everybody, then said," yo, thun that nigger Head thinks he's slick, he been getting over on us." They all worked on the block for Head.

Head had the pj's in a smash, but Carlos and DS didn't like Head, they thought he was pussy, because of some of the things he did.

This was at the height of the crack era, all the dealers knew it was big money to be made working in any projects.

With Queensbridge being one of the biggest one, there was drama all the time. We were having a shoot out with some dudes from the Bx for like two weeks for that nigga Head, and then he deaded the beef and gave them half of the projects to work on.

DS and Carlos didn't like that shit, there were many casualties for that war and it will take a lot for us to stand back now and do nothing about it, all because he said so. Three of our comrades Sly, Tree and Nut were locked up for killing an innocent bystander, because of it.

DS's girl Wanda got caught in the cross fire from the shoot out which took place in front of the 24-hour store. She got shot in her leg.

Carlos mind was running he had his concerns about Head, Carlos asked him," what's the deal with that dude, what did he do now, and how is he playing us?" DS was like," yo, we be going to the mill for him, bagging up three pies and he never pays us for that, we handle all the drama for that nigger, but he's paying Chip and Tank more than us and they get paper for bagging up. He wouldn't teach us how to cook up, it's like he wants us to be under him forever." Carlos said," word! Fuck that nigger I think it's time we made some real moves." DS was like," that's why I came to holler at u, you know R just got out, he told me he got the connect and knows how to cook up, he's just waiting for us." Carlos said," I didn't know sun was home, so he beat that Attempt. On police?" DS was like hell yeah, he had this ill lawyer, five-o just jumped out on him with their guns drawn and didn't identify their self as police officers. Sun just got shot in the arm two days before that for his diamond chain, he didn't know who they were, so he started blasting at them. He wouldn't of beat it, if he would of shot one of them, word! He just got 2 years for a gun charge and they didn't even catch him with one."

Carlos said," that's real, when are we going to kick it?" DS," I'll beep u later or in the morning." Carlos said," cool, I'll call u right back, just hit me." DS," y'all alright, got gats with y'all." Carlos said," of course sun, you know how me and L roll. Like that American express commercial never leaves home without it." They both laughed, DS gave him a pound and hug then said," I'm out of here, going to see Wanda, I'll hit u later." Carlos said," Alright sun peace." DS went to show everybody love, than walked out the park across the street to the projects. DS always had his hair in cornbraids. He only had one girl, didn't drink or smoke. His motto was u always had to be on point in the hood, u never knew what was going to happen and when.

DS stayed diesel at 5'3 and 185 pounds, it didn't matter what he ate, and he never gained an ounce. Just when DS walked off, this orange and blue housing cop car pulled up. Out of the driver's door, got out this cop we all called Rambo, after that Sly Stallone flick. He was 6'10, and built like Sly was in that flick. He was a real asshole, the whole projects hated that prick. He was a real racist motherfucker. Once he caught this 9-year-old kid taking a piss in the building. Rambo put the kids face in his own urine, and then cleaned up the piss by swinging the kid around in it, like a mop.

Rambo walked over to where the deejay Marly Marl was spinning two JVC 1200's and told him to cut the fucking music off now. Marly Marl did as he was told. Rambo said," u assholes got to 9:30, than that's it." L screamed from the crowd," fuck u dick head." Rambo didn't know who said it, he was fuming mad, and that caught him off guard. He said," come and say that in my face if you're man enough." His face was apple red. The whole park started laughing. The cops that was with him said," u fucking jungle bunnies got to 9:30 or you'll see what will happen." He than told his partner," let's go." Both of them walked back to their car and drove off. As soon as they were out of sight, Marly Marl started to play music again.

Carlos started to dance with this girl named Donna, she was all over him. After they finished dancing, they talked for a while, she gave him her phone number, told him to call her tonight. He looked at his Fendi watch, it was 10 to 8. He called Shakim and L," yo, I'm going to the block to start my shift." Shakim said," y'all go ahead, I'm not staying there watching u and L pump all night, see y'all tomorrow at the game." L said," cool!" Shakim said," be safe out here." They all exchanged pounds and Carlos and L walked off, they went to see Head.

Chapter 3

Head had on the newest Gucci sneakers, white guess shorts and a green polo shirt. Head was diesel, he worked out all the time. He was raised by his father Mack, his mother died when he was born from childbirth complications. Mack was a heavy heroin addict, he would steal from only the top of the line stores, B. Altman's, Macy's, Lord & Taylor, Gucci and stores in of that caliber. He would always go to Blue with all of the exquisite stuff and sell it to him for drugs and a little cash.

Mack died of an overdose, they found him on the roof in one of the buildings. Blue took Head under his wing, taught him the game. When things started to get hot for Blue, he sent Head to the army. In the Army, Head got a dishonorable discharge for breaking somebody's nose in a bar fight in Italy, and did some time over there for that. Once he got back to the hood, he took old man Blue's spot.

Blue is an OG (original gangster) always dressed in Armani suits and gators, even when it was hot out, he was dressed to kill. When Blue was in the drug trade, wasn't nothing being moved without him getting a piece. Blue's brother was a cold-blooded killer, everybody in the hood called him Satan. Blue was a smart hustler, he opened a few grocery stores, not only in the hood, but also in the Bronx, Brooklyn and upstate New York. He's heavy into the numbers running game now, that he passed the drug trade to Head, when he got out of the Army.

Head said," what's up youngen?" L said," ain't shit, ready to get my hustle on." Carlos's emotions were mixed up, cause of what DS told him in the park, but he couldn't let Head sense anything was wrong. Carlos said," what's the deal, ready to make moves." Head was looking right at him, seemed like he could see what Carlos was thinking. He said," come on, let's go get the work for tonight." Head had mad keys, like he was a building porter or something. Head had two cribs in every one of the 96 buildings out there, you never knew which apartment you were going to until, he brought you there.

They started walking with Head leading the way. Head said," Los, I seen your moms at the park, she hit me off with a fat plate, that shit was banging too." Carlos said," word we ate there too, that Mac and cheese ooh." L said," I wanted to get another plate for later." Carlos and Head said," Word!" at the same time. They laughed. We all walked across the basketball courts to 12th street. We were heading to Tisha's apartment. Tisha was mad cool, dark skinned, long hair, a model face and the body to match. She was one of Head's girls. L had a crush on her, once L asked her to go out. She went and told Head, Head flipped out, he was about to fuck L up. Luckily Carlos was there when it was about to go down. Carlos stopped Head, Carlos was holding him, Carlos said," yo, chill he didn't mean nothing by that, with all of your girls he didn't think you would miss one." Carlos added that for some humor anything to help defuse the situation some. Head started laughing about his comment, he felt like a pimp or something, he calmed down.

Carlos let him go, Head walked up to L put his finger in his face and said, don't u ever say anything to any of my girls, not hello or nothing, take this as a warning because the next time nobody's going to save your ass from me." L didn't say anything, just walked away feeling hurt and disrespected. Later that day Carlos called L's grandmother's crib to talk to him. Carlos told him not to worry about that, things are going to change real soon, just believe in him. Head told L," wait in front of the building." Head didn't bring L up to Tisha's crib anymore, because of what happened. L was like," alright, y'all hurry up though." Head angrily said," just look the fuck out for five-o and wait." Tisha's crib was on the fifth floor. Head always walked up the stairs, he never rode the elevator. Carlos was a little tipsy from the 40's, he drank at the park. When they got there, Carlos asked Head," why don't u ever take elevators?" getting his wind back. Head grinned, then said," you're never suppose to take the elevator, you've got to see who's in front of u and who's in the back. What will happen if u got off the elevator and the police was waiting for u, or even worse somebody u got drama with? It's going to be ugly." Carlos said," that's real, never thought about that." Head said," Los on the real, u got to be more conscious of everything out here, one slip you're dead or in jail." Carlos said," true, I'm always on point", then pulled out his 45 with two 12 shot clips. Head said," you're a wild lil nigga, put that away and let's get to business."

Head walked to the back room, Tisha's crib was fly. Wall to wall carpet, a 5,000-dollar entertainment center, marble tables, and the works. Her crib looked out of place in the hood, looked like all of this stuff belonged someplace else. Tisha was sitting down on the leather sofa-watching wheel of fortune, Carlos went and sat next to her, he said," Tis what's up lady? When are u going to stop playing and put me on to your cousin Tracy?" Tisha made a face that said it all, she rolled her eyes at him then said," Carlos u know I'm not going to mess her life up, by inducing the two of u." Carlos said," why not? Am I ugly or something?" Tisha said," no I'm not saying that, you look good, but all of that shit you're into, she doesn't need that in her life right now." Tisha looked right in his eyes than continued with," besides all u want to do is fuck her!" She waited to see how Carlos was going to react to what she said. His eyes didn't change, he knew the eyes were the windows to the soul and said," it's not like that, I been seeing her, I think she's the bomb and I really want to get to know her." Before he could get to finish talking Head yelled out," Los come in the back." Carlos told Tisha he'll holler at her later about that. She said," alright!" He went to the back room, in there was a king size waterbed, a nice ass bedroom set and the TV was hanging from the wall. Head gave him a brown paper bag, then said," you take $7,500, give L $2,000 and bring DS the rest, I spoke to him already, he'll meet u by your sister's building." Carlos said," cool, I'll do that right now." Head said," Los, I heard u talking to Tisha, her cousin likes u, step to her on your own." Carlos smiled," word, I'm going to see her tomorrow, I always see her coming from the train station, I know her time schedule and everything." Head laughed," you be clocking her hard sun, forget about that now, be safe out there, stay focused and watch them niggas backs." Carlos said," no doubt, I'm their eyes, I got eyes in the front and back, I'm Audi see you later."

Head walked with him back to the front and bent down over to kiss Tisha. Carlos told Tisha," I'll see you later and stop fronting on me about that." Then he winked at her. She smiled and said," Carlos go ahead with that." Then waved her perfectly manicured hands at him and added," be safe out there." Head looked out the peephole, after seeing no one was there he unlocked the door.

Chapter 4

Carlos walked back down the stairs, from that day on he never took an elevator in any projects again. When he got to the second floor window he stopped, looked out and yelled at L," is everything cool?" L said," yeah, hurry the fuck up, I been waiting for you for like 30 minutes." Carlos walked out the lobby, L was on the bench talking to Kiesha. Kiesha is a bonafide, bodacious, fine ass girl. Carlos walked over to them and said," Hi Key, what's up with Tray? If he needs anything, just let me know." Kiesha said," L just gave me $200 for him, so when I bring him the money I can bring his boots and army coat up there too. I'm going to go see him on Sunday, they moved him again, they put him in Comstock for cutting somebody, Poppy and Trip is in there with him." Carlos said," sun don't be playing no games u know that!" Carlos reached in his pocket and gave her three $100 dollar bills, to make sure everything was all right. Carlos said," Key see u later, me and L got to bounce now."

By time me and L got to his sister's crib DS was already there, playing Donkey Kong on an Atari 2600 with his nephew. Carlos split the work up just like Head told him too. Carlos told DS what Kiesha said about Tray. DS said," Tray blew that fiend ass nigga Will's head off last summer, that's good for him, shouldn't be trying to rob niggas" and laughed.

Will was an ex-boxer, who won the golden gloves championship two years in a row, but his addiction to heroin and crack got him suspended from fighting. So to support his habits, he went on a robbing spree, robbing everything, stores, old ladies and men, and he especially like to rob drug dealers, so he didn't have to go looking for a hit. Tray sold $10 and $20 dollar bags of heroin, one night Will went and copped a $10 bag from him, so he could make sure it was good enough to try and take. An hour later, after Will cooked up and shot the bag, he was high. He went back to Tray and hit him in his head with a baseball bat. Tray screamed out in pain, then fell, his head was busted wide open. Will dropped the bat with greed in his eyes and tried to reach into Tray's pocket. Before he could do that, Tray pulled out a 32 automatic and shot Will in the nuts. Will fell over screaming and yelling," please don't kill me." Tray got up and shot Will twice in the head.

Somebody saw the whole thing out the window and called the police. In the hood someone's always looking out the projects window. Tray's head was busted and bleeding, so bad he had to go to the hospital. Tray needed 100 staples inside and out, the scar ran from the bridge of his nose and ended at his hairline. Tray got knocked at the hospital, he got 7 to 14 for what I would call self-defense. Shit somebody wants to rob you and bust your head wide open then you have the right to shoot their ass. Will's robbery and drug arrest record went back to the early 70's, guess that's why Tray only got 7 years. Shit all the wrong that nigga was doing its like he did society a favor. We all bounced from his sister's crib, DS went to Wanda's house, L went to his grandmother's crib and I went on the block.

Troy was standing there with Ebony and Debbie. Troy started as soon as Carlos got over to him," Los it's 9 o'clock you're an hour late. Carlos gave Ebony two gee packs of dime vials and said," be easy Troy, I was with Head getting shit right." Troy said," I'm ready to go to Latin Quarters with Frenchie and them, I know they're mad at me cause I was pose to meet them at 8, next time do that shit earlier!" Carlos said," tell that shit to Head not me!" Troy gave Carlos a pound, lit up his coke-laced Newport and then started walking towards the Ave. Carlos yelled at him," u need to stop smoking that shit." Troy took a deep pull from his coke cigarette and said," fuck u nigga, u don't know what you're missing." Carlos said," I know this if u keep smoking that shit you'll become a crack head!" Troy said," are you crazy, never that!" and laughed, as he walked off the block. Troy was a crazy lil nigga. He had that napoleon complex, he was 5ft, 110 pounds. Troy just got out of jail for killing a cab driver. He was 14 years old at the time, now he was 18 years old. That was the longest they could keep him, because of his age. His cousin was with him, when it happened, he took the weight, he was 17 years old, and he got a 10 to 20. Troy beat all of his girlfriends up, he got a kick out of that sick shit. All the girls from around the way knew that, but still messed with him anyway. Carlos went to talk to Ebony, she was light skin, a little over weight, but she had a cute face. Ebony was a down ass bitch, she was wearing this hot ass Fila suit and the sneakers to match. Doorknocker earrings with her name between them, a gold and diamond name plate, rings on all her fingers and six bracelets on each arm. Carlos said," what's up Ebony? I know I'm late that shit wont happen tomorrow you got my word or I'll beep you if I'm late, alright?" Ebony said," I'm not sweating it, just glad you got here, that nigga Troy is always trying to talk to me, like I want his coke head ass." They both fell over in laughter, Carlos said," Troy is a good dude, he just needs to stop fucking with that shit." Ebony said," word, he be making mad chips, but he just sniffs and smokes it up." Carlos said," I know, its fucked up he's like my brother, can't see him go out like that, I'm going to check him in the a.m. about that, he thinks that shit is a joke."

Ebony and him could talk about anything, that's what he liked the most about her, anything they discussed stayed right there. I knew she liked me, but I told her let's just be friends'. After that, they stayed tight, it seemed like that made their friendship stronger. Everybody in the hood thought she was his girl, because they were together every night. They just pumped with one another, once they even slept in the same bed and nothing took place. Carlos told Ebony," I'm going to the store to get some beers, you want anything?" Ebony smiled then said," just make sure you get some cups, I'm not a chicken head who drinks out the bottle." Carlos said," most definitely." Before he left, he told Darren," watch Ebony's back, I'm going to the store u need something?" Darren said," Nah, I'm cool." Darren watched the other side of the block for us, so the cops couldn't creep up on us. The police think they're so slick, sometimes they tried to cross the roof on us. That's why we watched both sides of the block, because the buildings were connected, you could go in one and come out the other, Darren stayed on one side, Ebony and Carlos the other.

Chapter 5

When Carlos was about to cross the street, this metallic and silver Ninja 750 flew by and just missed him. Carlos put his hand on the 45 and said," watch wear the fuck you're going." The bike slowed down and pulled over, Carlos pulled his gat out, the dude on the bike pulled off his helmet. It was Jewel his brother, Carlos put the gun away and walked over to him and said," son you better stop playing like that, I didn't know who u was." He just starts to laugh and said," Los you're mad paranoid, u was scared to death." Carlos said," Hell no nigga, I was about to let the bullets start flying."

Jewel said," what's the deal?" Carlos said," ain't shit, we got's to poly, I'll call u after I talk to DS." Jewel said," do that, I'll see u later." Then wheeled off. Carlos thought fuck the store, I'm going to get on the job. His brother Jewel was a thug, at the young age of 12, him and Pop robbed Mr. James the local frankfurter truck man. Mr. James lived in the building next to mines. He closed the stand at 8 o'clock every night. He would have Shanita his retarded daughter, help him with all of the unsold goods. One day Jewel and Pop followed her and pushed her in the apartment. Duct taped her and locked her in closet. Cut all of the lights out, grabbed a metal lamp and hid behind the entrance door. Mr. James came in, before he could reach for the light switch,

Jewel knocked him out with the lamp. Pop and Jewel took everything they could carry out of the crib.

He got knocked for that three days later. He did four years for that, but when he got out, he went right back to crime and pulled off two more armed robberies. When he got out the last time, I put him on to Head. Head liked having wild niggas on his team, so he let Jewel run 40 Ave and 12th street. Plus Head knew that Jewel and his little devious cousin Pop was co-defendants.

Chapter 6

I went back to the block, Ebony finished the pack of vials I gave her, and so I went to get more.

Crack fiends were rushing the block, they sold all of the work Head gave Carlos, by the time L and DS came.

DS said," Los u had a good night huh?" Carlos said," Yeah, I pumped $8,500, call me tomorrow so I get ready for the game, we can go shopping." DS was like," alright, I'm going shopping with u, so we can talk." Carlos gave DS and L a pound and went to his sister's house to go to sleep. In the middle of his sleep, he had the weirdest dream, he dreamt he was standing in front of this big church cover in blood. He looked down and had this gigantic hole in his chest, when he seen it, he fell down, all the people in the church ran out. Standing over him talking gibberish were people he didn't see in a long time. This big light came, and he woke up in a cold sweat, the bed was wet like somebody threw a pail of water on it.

He got up changed the sheets and got in the shower. When he got up, he put on a Nike short set, red and black pair of Jordan's, and some polo sunglasses. He beeped DS, and then went to play with his nephew, his sister was making him something to eat. About 15 minutes later DS called back," yo, I'm on the corner waiting for u hurry up." Carlos said," okay, I'm coming right now." He went outside the sun was beaming, it was hot and humid. The hood looked so peacefully in the daytime, but he knew a disaster was waiting you could feel it in the air.

DS pulled up in a gold 525 BMW brand new. DS," get in sun, where do u want to go shopping at?" Carlos said," just take me to Steinway." DS said," u always go to Steinway, the whole hood goes there, and you're going to be looking like everybody else." Carlos said," I know but I don't feel like going to the city today, it's baking." DS," word! It's hot today." Carlos said," did u eat yet, let's go to Bel Aire's dinner?" DS," nah, I'm hungry, but first I'm going to pick up R."

R was a Dominican slim build guy, he use to live in Westchester County in a luxurious house, with a swimming pool, tennis court and everything. His father Raymond was a big time dealer on 151st and Broadway, he got caught by the DEA for conspiracy to sell 50 kilos and his whole organization went down. The DEA seized his house, cars and all of their belongings. His few friends that didn't get caught, promised to take care of his family, not one of them gave them a dime. Homeless with only the clothes on their backs, his moms went to the shelter, and later they were placed in Queensbridge. On the weekends R always went back to 151 street, against his mothers wishes. One of his fathers old friends asked him to delivery a package for him for $500 dollars, R got caught jumping the turnstile with the package, he was sent to juvenile hall, that's where him and DS became tight.

DS pulled over at 40 Ave and 21 street, R was on the pay phone talking. He put his hand up to signal us to wait. R hung up the phone and got in the car. R," DS, Carlos what's up? Put the ac on it's hot." They both gave him five, DS rolled up the windows and put on Boogie Down Production. DS drove to the diner, which was about 15 blocks from the hood, he parked in the front and they went in. This fine ass waitress sat us down, we chose to sit in the back so nobody could hear us talk.

R said," y'all ready to make this happen or what?" Carlos said," I'm with anything that's going to help me prosper, I'm ready to take it to the next level and get rich.' DS said," the only way that is going to happen, is we gots to clean house." R said," I got 5 mac-10's and a few 21 shot glocks, let's slay them niggas and take the whole hood." DS said," fuck Head and Tiny, all Head got is us and his cousin Poppy, and he'll be home in two weeks. We gots to hit him first that nigga will bust his gun." R said," what's up with OG Blue, is he going to get involved?" Carlos said," nah, I overheard him and Head talking one day, he told Head if anything ever happens, he's not involved. You see he didn't do anything with Tiny and them besides ain't anybody going to know what happened, but us at this table. People could think all they want too, first Tiny then Head and Pop." R said," I got the connect for all the drugs we need, so that's not a problem. My man knows where Tiny lays his head, once we hit him, his crew aren't coming to the hood no more, shoot the head and the body dies." Tiny was this Jamaican dude that ran the Bx crew. Carlos said," my cousin steals cars, we'll get a car from him and hit Tiny, whenever y'all are ready." DS said," I'm ready now, but we can't make no mistakes, murder is a slow process, we gots to map everything out than move." R said," just hold it down, we're going to do this right." The waitress came with three glasses of water, she asked," are y'all ready to order or do y'all need more time? DS said," we're ready." He ordered a tuna sandwich with a vanilla milkshake. R ordered a piece of carrot cake and a cup of milk. Carlos ordered French toast, two eggs, bacon and an iced tea. She went to put the order in they started back plotting. R said," I'm going to get three bricks all we gots to do is get $15,000 together and owe the rest. That's $5,000 a piece, the bricks cost $20,000 for each one. So we'll owe $45,000. DS said," we be making like 20 a day for Head, with him and Tiny out the way, we'll pay that in no time." Carlos said," word! Let's start putting this into action." The waitress brought our food, we ate, paid the bill then left. R knew of a person like Head's mentality it was to keep them needing you, don't expose your hand, feed them little jewels just enough for them to think you are teaching them something, pay them, give them gifts, make them feel loved. Most of the dudes in the hood was father-less, they were just looking for a father figure. That's how he kept them in a workers state of mind.

Chapter 7

Once they got to Steinway, DS parked in the parking lot, they all went to different stores. Carlos went to Dr. Jay's brought two pairs of guess shorts and three polo shirts. Then he went to Eternity's to get some sneakers and in the store he sees his man Don from the woods that's the next projects over. There are three projects that are close together Queensbridge, Ravenswood and Astoria. Don said," Los, what's going on son?" Carlos said," ain't shit just trying to keep my head above water, are u playing in the game today?" Don said," of course, we're going to beat y'all by 20." Carlos starts laughing," u wish that, better stop dreaming!" Don said," you'll see." Carlos said," on the real, I got some moves in the making, I'll get at you later." Don said," Okay, you got my new number?" Carlos said," nah, get a pen and give it to me." Don," hold on."

Don and him was cool, they went to Sterling together. Don and a few dudes had their projects hustle in smash, he had a high volume hair and nail salon in far rockaway. Don came back we exchanged numbers and Don said," just call me, whenever you need me I'm there!" Carlos said," you do the same, see u later at the game, hope you're ready to get your ass cracked." Don said," yeah right, we'll see who's the shit on the courts, I'll be sure to have mercy on you, because you're my man." And grinned. They gave one another a pound and he left. Carlos brought one pair of shell toe Adidas and some Stan Smith's. He walked to the car, DS and R was sitting there listening to music, Carlos got in, they drove back to the hood. They all got out, he gave DS and R a five and said," I'm going to get ready for the game, see y'all there. R are you going to play with us?" R said," nah, sun I don't play no sports or any games, strictly M and M., money and murder." DS laughed," yeah ok peace kid, see u later."

Carlos went to his mother's house to put his bags away and to change. She was in the kitchen washing dishes, she said," are u playing today? If not I'm not going out there it's too hot, I rather just sit here under the ac." Carlos said," yeah, I'm playing at 3:00, so make sure you're there to support me." She said," don't I always support your ass, I'll be there you better not make me look bad." Carlos said," you know, I'm going to do my thing." He went and put on his lucky basketball sneakers and changed his shorts and shirt. Carlos started to walk down stairs he was headed to the court. The block was crowded. Little kids on skates, jumping rope and running around playing tag, catch one catch all, all the childhood games. Miss Johnson and her crowd were sitting on the first role of benches to get a good view of the court. All of the girls came out too. Head gave a big tournament every summer, he supplied all of the equipment. The deejay, shirts, shorts, food, toys for the kids, and the 6 feet trophies for the winners. The MPV prize was an all-inclusive trip to Virginia Beach for two and a 7-foot trophy. Head gave the tournament in the honor of his niece who died from heart problems, while playing basketball four years ago.

Carlos spotted Head and went to his bench, Yogi the team's coach, gave him his shirt, number 7. Carlos always had that number every year. He put the shirt on, when he was pulling the shirt down he saw Tracy and Tisha coming in the block. She was wearing a yellow Chanel dress, black shoes and a black Chanel pocketbook. Tracy had a fat ass, washboard stomach, 32-cup breast, she looked like Tisha but her ass was a lot bigger. She went to John Jay College on an academic scholarship, her schedule was tight, and after school she worked at Rite Aid. He saw her look his way, he gestured for her to come to the sideline of the court. She started walking they met there, Carlos said," Tracy how's things going? And how's the family?" She said," everybody is fine! How's things on your end." Carlos said," things are good, but it would be a whole lot better if u let me take u out tonight!" She smiled," I have to think about that, I'll tell u later." Carlos said," I'll talk to u after the game." She said," sure." Then walked off, he was frozen there, looking at her.

Yogi called me back to the bench. Our starting five was Me, L, Shakim and the Cordell brothers Rob and Barry. Rob was here for the summer recess from the University of North Carolina, he's an all American star, last year he lead the country in scoring, he also was a running back for their football team. Barry plays for Yugoslavia overseas. The other team was Don, Lucky, Tyrone, Jermaine, and Shawn. We were equally matched for the championship game. The first half of the game was rough, Rob got most of the rebounds, and Barry, me and L did most of the scoring for us. Don and Lucky were the best players for their team. By the fourth quarter we were up by five, the score was 94 to 99. Five minutes left on the clock and he brought the ball up court, Shawn was defending him. Carlos faked right Shawn went for the ball, he crossed over, drove fast to the left lane and passed the ball to Barry, who two handedly dunked right in Tyrone's face. The crowd erupted, we beat them by two points. The final score was 110 to 108. Barry got the MPV, we got the gold.

After the game, we celebrated by eating and drinking. Carlos walked over to where Tracy and Tisha were sitting. She said," good game, I didn't know u could play that good." Carlos smiled," thank u" then handed her his trophy. She said," I can't take that, u worked hard for that." Carlos said," nah, it's okay I want you to have it." She said," Thank you."

He said," Can I get that movie date or what?" She smiled and replied," what time?" He said," here's my phone number, go get the newspaper find what you what to see, then call me. I'm going to shower and change." She said," okay I'm going to do that now." And walked towards the store. He went to see his moms and aunt and said," mommy I told you, I would do my thing." She said," you did good out there." She kissed his cheek, Carlos said," thanks, I'm going to get cleaned up and I will see y'all later."

Chapter 8

Carlos started walking to his sister's building when R called out," yo, Los wait up." Carlos waited for him. R said," good game, yo by next week we're going to put our plan in affect, u ready?" Carlos said," I'm ready, u got to get them Mac's to us." R said," come by later, I'll hit u off!" Carlos said," cool, I'm going to take a shower, I'll come see u in a few." R said," make sure u come to my block, peace!"

Carlos went upstairs, his brother was in his room with the door locked. Carlos had his own room at his sister's and mother's house. Carlos shook and banged on the door and said," Jewel open the fucking door, what are you doing in there?" Jewel said," hold the fuck up sun!" Carlos heard fast movement behind the shut door, Carlos pulled out his key to open the door, out comes Jewel and Tomeika. Carlos started dying laughing," yo, I know you wasn't fucking that hoe ass bitch in my bed?" She pushed pass him, her face all twisted up. Jewel said," don't call her no bitch" and grabbed him playfully. She walked towards the apartment door, before she could get all the way out, Carlos said," u stinking hoe, you need to use some summer love douche and wash down there!" She said," Fuck u!" and slammed the door. Carlos and Jewel both laughed, he went to lock the door and looked out the peephole. He said," wonder if she heard me laughing." Carlos said," fuck that chick." He said," nah sun, I might want to bone her again, I don't want her to hate me." And smiled. Carlos said," yo, change my sheets and flip the mattress over." Jewel went to the closet and started to clean up the room. Carlos went to the bathroom to shower, than he put on his Gucci sneakers, his new polo shirt and shorts. Jewel was sitting down watching a preseason NFL game, Greenbay and Miami. Carlos sat next to him and told him what him, DS and R was plotting. Jewel said," I'm with it, I don't like the fact that niggas from the Bx are out here hustling, we couldn't go to none of the projects out there. That shit wouldn't be that easy.

Poppy is my man, me and him was going back to back in C-74 and Elmira, but I know he's not going to let anything happen to Head, so he gots to get it. Head's time is up, he played himself." Carlos said," Word!" before he could say anything else the phone rang. Jewel jumped off the couch fast and grabbed the phone. Jewel asked," who do what to speak to? Hold on, it's for you." Carlos went to the phone," hello!" A female's voice, so sexy, like an Anita Baker song, said," are u ready the movie starts at 7:30?"He said," Tracy!" She said," yes!" he said," you sound so different over the phone, I'll meet you by Tisha's building." She said," okay." They both said," bye." and hung up. Carlos knew he had to pump at 8:00, so he called DS, on the second ring he picked up. DS," Yeah!" Carlos said." Yo, this is Los, I need u to hold the block down for me tonight and I'll do your shift in the morning." DS said." Sure I wasn't doing nothing anyway, Wanda went to Atlanta to visit her aunt." Carlos said." Good looking! I'm going to take Tracy to the movies and out to eat tonight." DS laughed and said." Finally nigga, about time, have a good time sun and don't trick all your paper on her on the first date." Carlos said." Come on sun with all of that nonsense, I'm not you, I'll tell u all about it, peace." Then he hung up, Carlos told Jewel "I'm out see u later." Jewel said," one love be safe."

Carlos went back to where Head was cooking out, he was on the grill flipping some burgers and franks. Head said," Los are you going to eat? Carlos said," nah I'm still full from earlier, Head is it cool if me and DS switch for tonight?" Head looked up," what the fuck do you want to switch for?" Carlos said," I wanted to take Tracy to the movies tonight." Head said," that's cool, you got her to go out with you? Yo but do that shit on your own time, cause every time she wants to do something with you after 8, you're going to want to switch and I hope you know it's not going down like that." Carlos seen the anger in his face, he just relaxed and said," nah, Head it's not going to be like that, just for tonight." Head said," u just, remember that." Carlos walked off, he was pissed, who does Head think he's talking to like that my father died years ago.

From that moment he knew Head's time was coming and fast. DS ran up on him, they started slap boxing. DS moved like a butterfly quick on his feet like a young Joe Louis, fast and deadly. Carlos on the other hand moved slowly like molasses, but when the slaps connected it was like being hit with an iron. They slapped boxed for like 20 minutes, both of them were winded, they walked to the store to get something to drink. Carlos asked DS," yo let me hold your car?" DS reached in his pocket without hesitation, gave him the keys and said," you know how I feel about my car, don't let anything happen to it and park in a parking lot." Carlos said," I got this, I'm not going to let nothing happen, my word is bond God." DS," alright Son, call me when u get back."

Carlos went to get Tracy, he called up to Tisha's window for her to come down. They went to DS's car, he always parked by the 24-hour bodega, so Moe could watch his car. Moe owned three of the eight bodegas in the hood. He was mad cool, but crazy too. He was from Libya, in his country they threw rocks at tanks and armed soldiers, so you know he wasn't scared of anything. DS paid him $150 dollars a week to watch his car over night. They got in the car, Carlos started to drive, he asked Tracy," Which movie theater are we going to and what are we going to see?" Tracy," to 42nd street and we're going to see Robo Cop." Carlos said," Oh, I thought we was going to see some love story, some girly shit!" Tracy said," what if I wanted to see something like that, you wasn't going to go?" He said," nah, truthfully I don't care what we see, as long as we're together." She smiled, we got on the 59th street Bridge to go to the city. He parked in a parking lot, two blocks from the theater. On their way to the flicks, they passed this Chinese man selling flowers, he brought her some red roses. She said," thank you, these are beautiful, I love red roses." He held her hand, when they got to the theater it was just starting. He went and got some popcorn and two drinks. They enjoyed the movie, and after they went to Beefsteak Charlie's to eat, and then he drove her home. She didn't live in the projects, she lived by Astoria Park, her parents had a nice house there. He parked, he asked her," if you live over here, why do I always see u in the pjs? She said," I go out there to check on my aunt, before I go to work." He said," Oh, I don't mean to be all in your biz, like that." She said," that's okay!" They talked for what seemed like hours about world news, schools, politics, music and everything that came to mind. She said," it's getting late I need my rest, here's my number call me tomorrow." They kissed and she hugged him, he waited for her to get in the house before he drove off.

Chapter 9

When he got back to the hood DS, Ebony and Darren was on the block. Carlos walked over, gave DS his car keys and said," everything alright?" DS said," it's cool, I'm just a little tried." Carlos said," I'm going upstairs to get some rest for the morning." He gave DS and Darren a five and hugged Ebony. For some reason he didn't have a nightmare again, he slept well that night.

Carlos got up at 7:00am, ate some fruit loops and made a peanut butter and jelly sandwich. He showered, brushed his teeth and got his self together. He went to the block, Head, DS and L was there talking. He walked over and gave them all a five. Head said," I got 40 tickets to the Fresh fest, Run-Dmc, BDP, Public Enemy, Eric b and Rakim, and somebody else in going to be there, Jay and Steve are going to run the block so we can all go, we'll meet up on 12th street at 7:00 pm." DS," yo, I need two tickets alright?" Head said," I got two for you, but not for no girls just niggas." DS said," nah, I need one for my man." Carlos said," Head u got one for Shakim?" Head," yeah! I'll see y'all later." And he walked off the block. DS told L to pardon us for a second, L went over to Fella his worker. DS said," Los go get that money, so R can get shit moving." Before he left he told L," I'll be right back, gotta run to my sister's crib." L said," go head, but hurry up."

DS and Carlos went to his sister's house, Carlos went in his room, he had this Adidas box filled with dough. He counted out $10,000, gave it to DS and then they left. Carlos walked DS to Wanda's house, he went to get his, and they went to R's crib. DS knocked on the door, R looked out the peephole, then opened the door. R said," come in and make yourself at home." R's crib was nice, but nothing like Tisha's crib. R went to his room and out came Gloria, she walked pass and went in the bathroom. R walked back to the living room, counted his paper in front of them, and then counted the sacks Carlos and DS gave him.

R said," yo, I'll have it first thing in the morning, and I'll hold on to this until, we take care of the little problem we have." DS said," Los get the car, we'll move on Tiny on Sunday, R put Gloria on him, he's going to take her out on Sunday, then she is going to get him to take her to the crib, we already know where he lives at, so u know what we're going to do, oh yeah R do u want to go to the concert tonight?" Carlos said," I'm going to call him now, R can I use the phone?" R said," go ahead Los, yeah I want to go to the concert! How did you get tickets?" DS said," from Head." and they both started laughing. Carlos dialed his cousin

Tony's number, he answered," hello." Carlos said," Tony it's Carlos, I need a car, something with four doors, its got to be took Sunday morning and make sure it's something fast." Tony," alright, I'll get u something fast, don't worry, but I'm going to need a few hundred, I'm hurting right now , u know I wouldn't charge you fam." Carlos said," I'll show love, don't sweat that, just make sure you get it, beep me when u do." Tony," no problem, I'll hit you, later." They hung up, Carlos told R," everything is all good on my end." R said," good hold up before y'all bounce." He went in the back and came out with two boxes, he gave DS and Carlos one. In the boxes was two brand new Mac-10's, both of them had two 32 shot clips and a box of Teflon 9 bullets. Gloria came out the bathroom with just a robe on and said," looks like y'all got some new toys." R said," Go back in the room." She just ignored him and went in the kitchen. Gloria was gorgeous, petite and innocent looking. She was Dominican like R, but her complexion was darker. She grew up with R, they were like the new Bonnie and Clyde. From the stories DS told him, she would go to all of the clubs and get the high rollers, the guys drinking the Moet and Don, with all the jewelry on to leave with her. She would bring them to a hotel and R and his click would rob them. Take everything, cars, jewelry, and leave them handcuffed in the room, with only their draws on. DS and Carlos left, DS said," Carlos come and get me before u go to the concert!" Carlos said," okay, take this box with u, I'm going to the block." They started on their way and by the time Carlos got to the block L was sitting on the bench. Carlos said," L what's the deal?" L said," shit was crazy a moment ago, the dees ran in the block, I thought they was coming at us, but they all ran in 40-15, they busted Chip's crib.. I'm hoping he didn't have nothing up there." Carlos said," word, that's fucked up, let's bounce from over here." L said," when Fella seen them coming he went to fiend Pam's crib." Carlos said," I'm going up there to tell him to chill, I know he's shaking like a leaf right now." L laughed and said," I know, I thought it was on for real!" Carlos went to Pam's apartment and knocked on the door. Pam opened the door the smell of crack residue and funk, rushed out the crib at him. Carlos took a step back, grab his nose and then went into the apartment. Carlos asked Pam," where the fuck is Fella at?" as he entered her studio apartment, there was like ten fiends in there. A few where sleeping on a mattress that was on the floor, others were at the table freebasing out of empty beer cans and 25 cent juices containers. The place smelled of death. She said," he's in the bathroom." Carlos walked past Pam to the bathroom and turned the doorknob but the door was locked. Carlos looked at Pam who weighted like 90 pounds her face was all sucked in from all the crack she smoked and knocked on the door. Fella open the door, then stepped back in the tub to look out the window, he said trembling," where the fuck they go?"

Carlos said," calm down sun, they kicked in Chip's crib, let's get the fuck out of here." He said," alright!" before they left Carlos told Pam," stop having all of these motherfuckers in here, let them come after the shift is over." Pam said," okay I'm sorry can I get a few please?" Carlos said," hell no didn't L hit you before we started today?" she said," yeah, but I'm thirsty just give me two and y'all don't have to pay me for tomorrow." Carlos said," Pam we always go thru this shit, I'm not feeling your bullshit today, just get these people out of here, than I'll give it to you later."

Fella and him was walking down the stairs, all they could hear is Pam breaking and kicking people out. When they got back downstairs L said," they all left, they took Chip and his girl with them." Carlos said," damn we're going to have to find out later what happened." L," I'll call his moms later to find out the deal."

Chapter 10

The rest of the day was smooth, after his shift was over Carlos went to Tisha's crib to see Head. Head was sleeping, she went to wake him up. Carlos gave him all the money they made and told him about Chip. Head said," wasn't nothing up there, but some weed and his gun, it's his first offense, he'll be home tomorrow." Carlos left and went to his mother's crib to get a few hours sleep before the concert. He must have over slept, because he felt DS and Shakim shaking him to get up. Carlos rolled over and said," just give me a few more seconds." Shakim flopped his fat ass on the bed, Carlos almost flew off, Shakim said," get your lazy ass out of the bed." and pushed Carlos's head. Carlos got up and went to the bathroom to get ready. DS was banging on the bathroom door telling him," Hurry up sun we're all waiting for u." Carlos yelled out," I'm coming damn." His mother was on the sofa laughing, he could hear her and Shakim talking. Carlos rushed to shower and to get dressed. We all walked to 12th street, the block was packed, everybody headed to the train station it was about 40 of us. Before Carlos got on the train he brought 20 packs of Gem razors and gave everybody one. The train ride was crazy, niggas was wilding, all of the people started to get off the train, thinking they was going to get robbed, but they wasn't on our minds tonight. As we approached Madison Square

Garden It was more like a riot than a show, niggas were wilding.

DS came home with 9 gold chains, he was cutting niggas. DS's man Shawn got robbed for his three finger ring and his gold fronts, he got lost in the crowd and ended up running into the same cats who took his shit. Lucky had to go back to the hood without a shirt, because his shirt was covered in so much of other people's blood. When we were leaving, DS, Lucky and L was snatching mad chains. They all got home safe, except Prince, Sky and Trevor they got arrested. When everybody got to the block Darren was sitting on the fence in front of his building. L and Carlos walked over to him," what happened wasn't u with us?" Darren said," yo, I went to piss, after I finished I tried to catch up to y'all but I couldn't find y'all, so I'm like fuck it I'll see y'all inside. I had my ticket in my hand four dudes ran up on me and took it, one of them punched me in my face. I saw this cop-walking pass, I told him these guys took my tickets. The officer asked me which one, I took him to the guy that hit me and the other three guys were behind the cop pointing with their fist telling me they was going to fuck me up. The cop asked me my seat number, I told him, the guy he grabbed pulled out a different ticket. He said there is nothing he can do because he didn't see him take it. He went to walk off, I asked him can he walk me to the train station, and he did, them niggas was laughing in my face, I was mad, there was nothing I could do, so I got on the train and came home." L and Carlos laughed at the story he told. L kept laughing and called DS over. L told Darren to tell DS the story, Darren retold the events as they occurred. When he was telling the part about him telling the police, Carlos saw DS facial expression change, his eyes got very small and beaded. Carlos knew when he did this, he was up at something. Just as Darren finished telling the tale, DS hit him with a right jab and a left hook. Darren fell back over the fence he was sitting on. He knocked him out cold. L hopped over the fence to help Darren, Carlos asked DS," what the fuck you do that for?" grabbing his arm. DS pushed his hand off of him and said," fuck that nigga going to the cops. It's niggas like him that will get us all life, he's telling about a free ticket, imagine how much telling he'll do if some real shit happened. I'm not with co-signing shit like that." And he walked off the block. Carlos went to help L pick Darren up, Darren's left eye was closed, his lip and the back of his head was busted. He was confused and disoriented, he didn't know where he was. He was asking us, "what happened?" Carlos leaned him against the fences and told him," you shouldn't be fucking with the police!" L walked Darren to his building, Carlos was exhausted after all this evening activities he went to get a good night's rest.

Carlos thought about what just took place, he felt sorry for Darren he was a good dude, but DS had a point. When you're out here struggling in these streets u can't show any signs of weakest, because in this concrete jungle the strong prey on the weak.

Chapter 11

Carlos went to the phone and dialed Tracy's house her father answered, then put her on the phone. They talked for a while, until he fell sleep. His nephew woke him up, his sister just brought his nephew home from day camp. Carlos hugged him and rubbed his head lightly, Carlos told him," give me a five." They both slapped hands, then he ran into his room, Carlos went to brush his teeth, sat on the sofa, turned on the TV set to watch the news. His nephew came and sat next to him," I want to watch cartoons!" Carlos turned to Bugs and Daffy, they both sat there and watched cartoons. The phone rang, his sister informed him that it was for him, Carlos asked who it was she told him DS. Carlos took the phone from her," what's up kid?" DS said," ain't shit, it's quiet today I just finished my shift, I'm on my way to see u, I called your mom's crib she told me, u was over here." Carlos told him to come upstairs. A few minutes later DS came in, he gave him a pound and said," yo, come with me to the gym?" Carlos said," Cool, just let me get my stuff together." Carlos put a sweat suit, a bar of soap, a towel, washcloth, his Walkman with his Al Green and Whispers tapes and his running shoes. He stuffed all of that into his gym bag, DS drove to the BQE racquetball and fitness club. He was a member there, and members was allowed to bring a guest for the fee of $10 dollars. They went to the locker room to change into to their gym clothes, they shared a locker because Carlos forgot to bring his combination lock. DS said," Los I didn't mean to push you last night, but that dude Darren is a meatball. I can't fuck with dudes of that caliber, this is the real world, and you can't justify any snitching on any level. Dudes like him are weak links, our chain has to be strong, and you know the weak link pops the chain. Just like Head once u show any signs of weakest in these streets, the wolfs are out to get you. How can we be around dudes like that and expect real niggas to respect us? So much depends on your reputation, guard it with your life" Carlos said," you're 100 percent right about that snitching shit, but I thought that shit was funny." DS smirked and said," it was funny, until he started that police shit." DS went and got on the treadmill, he started to jog. Carlos did a lightweight chest and back work out. They worked out for an hour, went to the steam room and after that they swam for a while. DS did some laps, Carlos was just swimming around flirting with these two girls that were in the pool with them. Carlos showered and changed to the other pair of shorts and tank top he brought with him, they went to the juice bar they had there and ordered him and DS a banana and strawberry drink. After they changed, they went back to the hood.

Chapter 12

DS parked by the 24-hour store, they walked to Carlos' block. Jewel, Chip, Troy and a few other dudes were playing cee-lo. Troy was standing there smoking his coke-laced Newport, his usual while shaking the dice in his hand. Troy had the bank, he was talking mad shit, his other hand was full with $20's, 100's and 50 dollars bills, and he didn't have any singles. Troy rolled three and two fives his point was three. Chip bends over and picked the dice up. Carlos said," Chip you're home? what happened sun?" Chip leaned up, shaking the dice over his head and said," Rambo and his crew ran up in my spot, fucked the crib up poured shampoo on all of my leathers, ripped my shirts up, did all types of foul shit. All they found was half of a blunt and this broke 22 I had. Rambo was going crazy at the precinct asking me all kinds of questions about everybody that was somebody in the hood. I told him the weed and gun was mines and I don't know nothing, they let my girl go, and my bail was $1,000 dollars, Tonya bailed me right out. Shit I'm trying to get that paper back right now!" He yelled," come on cee-lo dice!" he rolled a two, three and six. Troy yelled," almost 123rd street!" Chip said," hell no! I need the 4,5 and 6 baby!" he picked up the dice and rolled again. Carlos told everybody," I'm outta here Peace." DS and Carlos left.

Carlos went to his mother's house to get something to eat, that work out had him exhausted and hungry. His mother was sitting on the sofa watching TV, Carlos said," What's up mommy?" She said," just relaxing watching the soap operas I taped earlier." he asked her," is there anything to eat?" she said," there's some leftover baked chicken, rice, black eye peas and greens in the refrigerator." Carlos ran in the kitchen, washed his hands, made a big plate, put it in the microwave and chowed down. After he finished, he went to his room and went to sleep. The sound of gunfire woke him up. Carlos pulled his blinds up and looked out of his bedroom window, everybody was running, screaming and going crazy. Carlos put on a pair of jeans and sneakers then took his 45 out of the dresser draw and went down stairs. There were two people lying on the floor, the sirens from the cop cars were blaring. Carlos told Kiesha to come in the lobby with him, he gave her the 45 and told her to put it in her pocketbook. They both walked back out the building to see what happened. Leeza, Tammy and Donna were on their knees, over Stacey holding her hands telling her not to move. Carlos looked, there was a big hole in Stacey's left shoulder, blood covered her shirt. Stacy was screaming and crying while trying to move, Donna held her down. Carlos could see she was in excruciation pain, the cops and paramedics rushed over. Carlos went to see whom the other person was it was Chip. Carlos saw it in his eyes that he wasn't going to make it. Carlos said," Chip hold on sun and be strong." His eyes were rolling back and forward, he was trying to stay awake. Rambo told the paramedics that someone else was hit, the paramedics put him on a stretcher and put him in the ambulance. Erica was telling this detective everything she knew, she seen Carlos looking at her, she went and sat in the cop's car. Troy walked over to Carlos, he had a sad look on his face. Carlos asked him," what the fuck happened?" he put his arm around his shoulder and moved him away from the earshot of everyone, all eyes were on them as they walked away. Troy said," Carlos we was all playing cee-lo, Chip was winning all of the money. He took the bank and $1,500 from me, I quit after that but I stayed there watching the game. Chip kept rolling cee-lo and head crack back to back, he had Jewel down $5,100. Jewel asked Chip for some walking money, Chip told him no. Jewel asked him was he sure about that, Chip said yeah, I'm not giving anybody anything. Jewel just walked off without saying anything. Jewel and Cash came back on bikes, I knew what time it was when him and Cash dropped the bikes and pulled out two big ass guns. They told everybody to empty all of their pockets, but Jewel told me to bounce. I started walking without looking back, all I heard was Cash saying I'm telling you don't try it, then the guns started going off. I jetted I guess Stacey got hit in the crossfire. Carlos said," damn that's fucked up, I told sun about that gambling shit!"

Troy and Carlos went to the store on 40 Ave and 10th street to get a six-pack of Heinekens and walked back to the block, the police had that side of the block taped off, so they went on the hill. As soon as they got to the other entrance Mrs. Davis (Chip's mother) was rushing by with Tonya (Chip's girl). Carlos asked Tonya," is Chip okay?" She replied angrily," don't you say a fucking thing to me, your brother did this shit, you motherfucker!" she tried to take a swing at him, he caught her arm then pushed her back. Carlos said," you better take it easy, I didn't do anything to you or him bitch!" Mrs. Davis wrapped her arm around her while they walked to a cab that was waiting for them.

Carlos could hear her still saying shit as she got in the car, he put his middle finger up at her as they drove off. Troy said," don't sweat that, she's upset right now." Carlos said," I'm not sweating that bitch, I know this she better stay the fuck out of my way." They went and sat at the card tables, Kiesha noticed them there and came over. Troy opened a beer for her as she sat with them. Carlos told her," bring that gat up stairs and go to the hospital to see how Chip and Stacey is doing, matter of fact hold up a second." He got up, went across the street to the public pay phone and called

DS. DS answered the phone on the fourth ring," hello." Carlos said," sun come to the hill I'm in front of Associated, bring the car around." DS," what's the deal sun I was sleeping." Carlos said," DS, I need to talk to u it's important, I don't want to talk on this jack." DS," I'm on my way, say no more!" They hung up, Carlos opened another beer and sat with Troy and Kiesha. Troy was sitting there with both of his hands rubbing his head, Carlos asked him if he was alright? Troy," yeah, I was just thinking about what happened." Carlos said," Hold your head sun, here's another beer" handing it to him. DS pulled up, Carlos went to his car, leaned on the passenger doorframe and told him what he knew so far. Carlos asked him," take me and Kiesha up to Elmhurst hospital?" He said," Come on let's go!" Carlos called Kiesha over, told her to get in the car, and gave Troy a pound and hug. Carlos said," Troy go up the crib, relax man I'll call u as soon as I find out something."

Carlos got back in the car. They drove up Northern Blvd. to Broadway. Carlos told DS to park down the block from the hospital and told Kiesha to go in and find out what's going on with Chip and Stacey, we'll be right here waiting for you. Carlos and DS sat there in silence with no radio playing. Kiesha got in the emergency room Mrs. Davis was just standing there, with a distance look in her eyes, Kiesha went to her," Mrs. Davis are you okay?" Mrs. Davis didn't answer,

Kiesha went to the double door to the waiting room. The hall was full with a lot of Stacey and Chip's friends. Tonya was crying uncontrollable, breathing hard in and out. Kiesha called Donna and Leeza over," How's Chip and Stacey doing?" Donna hugged Kiesha, broke down in tears and said," Kiesha, Chip is dead they tried to save him, but they couldn't, Stacey is in surgery her collar bone is shattered, the doctors said she's going to be okay." Tears came to Kiesha's eyes, she tried her best to hold them back, but couldn't. She told Donna, she needed some air, and walked back through the doors and back to the car.

Looking out the front windshield, Carlos saw Kiesha coming, it hit him, he knew the inevitable, without her saying a word to him, and he knew Chip died. She opened the back door and got in, she said," Jewel and Cash killed Chip, Stacey is in stable condition." That was all that was said on the ride home, Carlos handed her some tissue from the glove compartment. Once they got back to the hood, Carlos told Kiesha," to bring that gat to her crib, I'll stop by later to get it." She said," okay, Carlos call me." And walked to her block. DS," damn Jewel gots to get low for while, we can hold him down with paper but he just can't come out here no more." Carlos said," true, I'm going to try to get in touch with him, good looking for taking us up to the hospital." DS said,"

come on sun that's nothing, you're my brother until we die."
They exchanged pounds, Carlos told him," I'll call him later"

Chapter 13

Carlos walked to the river park to clear his thoughts, when he got there he went down to the river, and leaned on the fence. Looking over the East River at the tall skyscrapers in Manhattan, his mind started to wander, thinking about Jewel, Chip, Stacey and Cash. Mr. Gray walked up on him tapping his shoulder, he turned around shocked and startled, he didn't see him in a year and a half. He asked," Mr. Gray what are u doing down here?" He said," I was going over some of the things I discussed today with a few students. I seen u walk by you didn't even notice us. I figured you was doing some heavy thinking, so I decided to walk over to see if I could help u ease your mind." Mr. Gray was a very educated brother, who believed in education and encouragement while trying to uplift our people. He talked about black owned business and things of that nature. He was a college teacher for a while, but he quit and became a financial advisor at Tyson and Son's. Soon after he opened a service for young adults, teaching them the ins and outs of the stock and bond market. His success on Wall Street made him a financial powerhouse. He worked and used his own capital to run the center, he always preached the youth are the future and he was here to guide them the right way. While teaching them about economics, business and ethical and social freedom.

Carlos said to him," I'm sorry I didn't say anything to u, but I got a lot on my mind so I came down here to think straight and get some mental direction." He said," that's the right thing to do, always think before you react. Carlos what have you been doing with yourself, are you in school or working?" Carlos said," nah Mr. Gray I'm on the block getting that money!" Mr. Gray," you need to go back to school, Carlos school education is way more important than street education. The shit you learn in the streets is pretty much illegal shit that don't lead to anything but trouble down the road. Only a few cats have been fortunate enough to become successful without a full rounded college education and they are truly blessed. The bottom line in life is, the more money you get, the smarter you have to get. You don't have to have any intelligence to be ass broke, but when you get $10 you gotta be smarter than the guy with $20 or he'll take it from you. Now what happens is, a dumb ass kid gets some money and he hires people around him who are intelligent. The people he hires take it from him, you hear that story all the time. It wasn't some gangster from the street that robbed him, it was the guy that worked for him, the one he hired because he didn't reevaluate the workers knowledge. I teach the kids all about the business world, so that will not happen to them. I think that no matter how much street education you get, you're going to have to get some book education, because once you manage real money.

The money is going to force you to learn, hopefully some street smarts will come in and allow you enough insight into knowing who you're dealing with.

I try to teach you young cats that don't think that real business is played the same way the drug game is played. For you'll to reach my level of business, you have to be educated, because you'll be engaging in something that's not controlled or run by street people, it's controlled and ran by college people. You gotta know what the fuck you're doing, I tell express how important it is to get smarter, read some books, learn about computers, and take courses, and most of all stay in school. Looking at the long-term effects between book smarts and street smarts, book smarts could get you to be a CEO of a company, be a doctor, anything you want. Street smarts can't get you nowhere, but the penitentiary. Take the street instinct and turn it over to the books and you can become a real powerful player. Carlos said," That's real deep Mr. Gray." He said," I just keep it real and tell the truth. Great minds discuss ideas, average minds discuss events, and small minds discuss people. Here's my card, come stop by I can help you get it together young brother." Carlos said," okay I'll give you a call." He said," its never to late, missed opportunity only comes by so often, think about it." He went back to his students, Carlos walked out the park back to his block.

Chapter 14

A few crowds gathered on his block talking about the latest gossip, Miss Johnson was out in her nightgown and some flip-flops gossiping amongst her friends, when Carlos walked by things got quiet, she put up her hand and waved at him. He just walked by acting liked he didn't see her. As he got to his mother's building detective Bundy and Collins were getting in their unmarked car. Carlos stood his distance, waited for them to pull off and was off the block before he went in the lobby of his building. He opened his mother's door, his sister was putting the water jug back in the refrigerator. She had a glass of water in her hand, they both went in their mother's room. His mother sat on her bed, her eyes were swollen and blood shot red. He knew she had just finished crying, his sister handed her two aspirins and the glass of water. She put the pills in her mouth and took a deep drink of water, then gave the glass back to her. His sister left them alone in the room, Carlos sat down beside her, put his arm around her shoulder and she put her head in his chest. Moments passed with not a said word, their embrace brought tears to his eyes. She got up gave him a tissue and went in her closet, pulled out a framed photo of Charlie (Chip) and Jason (Jewel). The picture was from when they were kids, with their St. Rita's softball uniforms, their arms was around each other, Jewel was holding a bat and Chip was holding the trophy they won that year. She handed me the picture and said," Carlos how could this happen? They once were friends, I know Jason was gone for a while, but this isn't right! Me and Mrs. Davis are good friends how can I look her in the face, knowing my son took her sons life over nothing?" He was lost of words, there was nothing he could have said to make things right.

Chapter 15

The day of Chip's funeral it was gloomy and raining. DS and L rented a Lincoln Town car limousine. The wake was 12 to 2 and the last viewing and funeral was 4 to 7. They chose to just go to the final viewing. Shakim, L, Gloria, R, Tracey, Wanda and Carlos met at 41 Ave and 10th street, DS pulled up and got out. DS, L, Shakim, R and Carlos were all dressed with nice shoes, slacks and white shirts with ties on. The girls were dressed elegant, they all had on nice black dresses. They all got in the limousine, the driver took them to Gilmore's Funeral home on Linden Blvd. They drove pass, the place was crowded, the driver parked in the lot. Carlos thought to his self a lot of people came out today, Chip will be greatly missed. L got out first and helped all of the ladies out of the car. DS and Carlos stood behind as everybody else walked to the funeral home, they watched as Wanda and them greeted everybody. Carlos said to DS," yo, I don't think I can go in there!" DS," it's not like y'all weren't peoples, him and Jewel just got into some shit. We lost two good niggas that night Chip to death and Jewel to a life on the run." Carlos said," I just feel out of place coming here, knowing what caused this!" DS," sun fuck everybody your here like a man to pay you're respect to Chip no one else. Let's just go in their pay our respects then leave if you're uncomfortable." They walked in the funeral home, Carlos could feel the cold stares from Tonya, pricking at his soul like cold daggers of ice. DS grabbed him by his shoulder and said," later for her Los." They walked to the casket, Chip looked like a mannequin of his former self, like his skin was covered in plastic. DS and Carlos kneeled down on the pew, they said a prayer for him, did a Hail Mary and got up to leave. Mrs. Davis called them over, gave them both a hug and said," I know this is uncomfortable for y'all as it is for me. I'm glad y'all came, I seen you boys grow up. I have a lot of pain and sorrow about this, but I forgive Jason for what happened the Lord will deal with him in his own way. It's hard for my heart to forgive him, but it's the Lord's teaching, so I have to deal with it. I prayed for Charles everyday to be carefully in them streets, but that's the life he chose. Everything is written by the Lord before it happens, I'm hoping something positive will come out of this, I hope it will change y'all ways. Please don't leave yet, I want y'all to hear the good word from the pastor." She kissed both of their cheeks, they went and sat in the last row of seats. The things she said to him had him on the edge of tears, DS and Carlos talked about the conversation with Mrs. Davis and realized she is a strong willed and forgiving woman, more than they ever imagined. The pastor motioned for everyone to sit down and to be quiet. He spoke with great passion," How's everyone today? I can't hear you, I know we're assembled here today to see Charles Davis on a peacefully journey home, it's not a time to be sad, it's a time to celebrate. Knowing that he is now in the forever-loving hands of Jesus Christ! This ceremony symbolize the going to a greater place for Mr. Davis, he is one of the rare jewels going to a place of no more suffering and eternal life, going to meet our father in heaven. Today I'm going to read a chapter from the book of Palms. When I call out, answer me, O God who vindicates me! Though I am hemmed in, you will lead me into a wide, open place. Have mercy on me and respond to my prayer! You men, how long will you try to turn my honor into shame? How long will you love what is worthless and search for what is deceptive? Realize that the Lord shows his faithful followers special favor, the Lord responds when I cry out to him. Tremble with fear and do not sin! Do some soul-searching as you lie in bed, and repent of your ways! Offer the prescribed sacrifices and trust in the Lord! Many say," Who can show us anything good?" Smile upon us, Lord! You make me happier than those who have abundant grain and wine. I will lie down and sleep peacefully, for you, Lord, make me safe and secure. A lot of the older people were saying," Amen and yes Lord." He continued," Listen to what I say, Lord! Carefully consider my complaint! Pay attention to my cry for help, my king my God, for I am praying to you! Lord, in the morning you will hear me, in the morning I will present my case to you and then wait expectantly for an answer. Certainly you are not a God who approves of evil, but may all who take shelter in you be happy! May they continually shout for joy! Shelter them, so that those who are loyal to you may rejoice! Certainly you reward the godly, Lord. Like a shield you protect them in your good favor! With prayers and deepest sympathy and God shall wipe away all tears from their eyes. Revelations 21:4. There is no limit to God's love, during your time of grief, take comfort in knowing that only he knows the reason for loss and he can heal our hearts of its sorrow. Everyone clapped he said," thank you please bow your heads so I can say a prayer for him." After he finished his emotional prayer, everyone said," Amen" The pastor said," please everyone remain seated, Sister Mary is going to sing a farewell song." Sister Mary cleared her throat and sang Amazing Grace first lowly, but clearly then she hit high notes so accurate, it sounded so lovely and sad at the same time. Tracey broke down in tears so did a lot of people in the audience. The deacon passed out Chip's obituaries to everyone, the pastor told everyone to make a line for the last viewing before the burial. Shakim, L, DS, R and Carlos went to say their last good-byes, and then went to the limousine to wait for Wanda, Tracey and Gloria. Once everybody got there DS said," I'm not going to the burial, so if anyone of y'all want to go find another ride!" Tracey said," that's all right DS me, Wanda, and Gloria are going to ride there with my cousin and Head. We'll see y'all in the projects." She came and put her arms around Carlos's waist, kissed him and then asked was he okay. Carlos said," I'm okay baby, beep me when y'all get back." They walked off and he got back in the limousine DS told the driver," back to Q.B.!" He took off his tie and said," that was some sad shit, may he rest in peace." R said," hold up before we leave" told the driver," to go around the corner and stop by that black car." R got out walked over to the passenger side window and was talking to whoever was inside. Shakim," who the hell is he talking too?" DS said," I don't know and don't care. Yo, Richie is coming home today, we have to pick him up at the Port Authority. That's why I didn't want to go to the burial and plus I had enough of this sad shit today!" Carlos poured a shot of vodka from the bar and said," Word! We're going to have a party tonight." The black car drove off, R got back in the limousine and told the driver," you can go now." Carlos asked him," who was that in the Benz?" He said," that was my peoples I told them to meet me here, just in case somebody tried to front" and flashed two nines," fuck that you're my man I'm not going to let nothing happen to you, I heard Chip's punk ass cousin was talking some funky shit. I hope he knows better, cause once he fakes a move he's going to join Chip in a casket. When I heard the shit he was talking, I was going to get him laid down, but I know he's a coward that's why I didn't say anything. I was in Harlem Valley (a youth correctional Facility) with him, he was washing niggas draws and shit like that. My man Tyheim from Fort Greene told me what was going on and I stepped to him told him you better rep the hood, tried to give him a banger to handle his biz, he would not take it, so I stopped fucking with him. But I don't sleep on nobody that's why I made sure we was right." He threw Shakim a White Owl blunt and told him to roll up. Carlos said," Good looking R but the next time let me know, I can hold myself down sun I bust my gun." R said," there's not a doubt about that! I was just looking out I knew you had mad shit on your mind, I didn't want to see you do nothing stupid."

Chapter 16

They got on the Grand Central Parkway, got off at Hoyt Ave, DS told the driver to go to Astoria Blvd and stop at Fishbein's liquor store. He went in the liquor store came out with a case of Moet. DS told the driver to take them to 8th street, he got out and went to the pay phone. Looking out the limousine's window, Carlos saw Knowledge, Freedom and Shaheim. He got out and went to talk to them. Knowledge said," Peace God! What's the deal God?" Carlos gave them all a pound and said," ain't shit we just came from Chip's wake and now we're going to pick up Richie." Freedom said," I heard about Chip, what's up with Jewel?" Carlos said," I don't know, I didn't speak to or see sun since that happened." He knew that Freedom was Jewel's man, they did a few heists together and Freedom would hold him down. Gary and two bitches walked up to DS they were talking. DS yelled," what's up Knowledge? Carlos let's bounce!" Carlos told Shahiem, Freedom and Knowledge, Peace, I'm out" and got back in the car. The two girls climbed in the back seat too. DS told the driver to take us to the Marriott by the airport. DS asked the girls," What's y'all names again?" The brown-skinned one said," Betty and my partner's name is Chance." DS said," my name is DS" pointed at Shakim," Shakim" then at Carlos," Los" and then R," Big R." We all shook hands, the driver pulled right up to the front of the hotel, and DS went to check in. Carlos said to Chance," y'all going to take care of my man or what?" Chance said," hell yeah, we're going to rock his world!" Carlos said," Show me something!" Chance grasped a hold of one of Betty's breast, they started kissing, and Betty opens her legs she had on this short mini-shirt without any underwear on. Chance put her finger inside of Betty's vagina, stroking it in and out slowly, Betty stopped kissing and said," yeah bitch do it like that!" Before the show could really get started, DS tapped the window and told them to get out. R said," yeah baby it's on now." Shakim was looking like a child in a toy store. DS gave Shakim the room key and told him," Go to the room 711, wait with them chicks until we get back and put the champagne on ice." We took out two bottles and gave it to them, Shakim jumped out the car smiling and started to walk to the hotel with them. L said," Hold up sun I'm coming with you!" and jogged to catch up to them. DS told the driver to take us to the Port Authority, the driver took the Mid-Town Tunnel to 34th street, went west to sixth Ave and made a right on 42nd street. DS," I don't drink, but today I'm going to drink with my boy Richie." They waited by the bus terminal, they got out the car, excited waiting for Richie. A dark blue Cutlass pulls up, Cash yells out the back window," Yeah niggers what's up" holding his hand out the window pretending to have a machine gun. R says," oh shit look at that stupid nigga!" The Cutlass pulls over and out the back doors comes Jewel and Cash. They walked to each other and all give each other pounds, they was celebrating like an old reunion. Carlos said to Jewel," why didn't you call me?" Jewel said," I know they be tapping phones and shit. That's why I didn't call mommy's house, I knew if I beep you, you would of most likely called from there. So I didn't risk it you know." Carlos said," Word that was good thinking." Jewel," I spoke to DS today, he told me to meet y'all up here." Carlos said," what the fuck happened?" Jewel," sun that nigga Chip took all of my money, then he wouldn't give me a dime back. If he would have given me $50 dollars or something that shit wouldn't have happened. He tried to reach on me, it was him or me, he lost sun. You know I didn't really like him anyway, he waited to I went to jail and was fucking with my bitch. I took $15,000 that day I brought a half of key, me and Cash are doing our thing in Manhattan. Sun I'm just trying to get this lawyer paper up." Carlos said," we gots to stay in touch, beep me and put in 40 after the number, that way I'll know it's you and I'll get right back in touch with you. Are u coming to the Marriott with us?" Jewel said," what room y'all in? I'll come by later." Carlos said," 711 the one by the airport." Jewel said," cool I'll be by later, I got to run and do something first."

Richie comes out of the terminal with two big brown paper bags in his hands. Richie is 6'6 and 280, he was big before he left, but now he was solid and huge. Richie was Puerto Rican, he had a small curly Afro. He walked over to us, one by one and we exchanged greetings. Carlos introduced him and R, DS told Jewel and Cash," we're out come to the room." Jewel and Cash got back in the Cutlass and drove off. Richie, R, and Carlos got back in the car, DS put the bags in the trunk, opened a bottle of champagne and poured everyone a glass. R told the driver," back to the room." DS sat down and slammed the door shut, Richie said," it's good to be home, 4 and a half years in that hellhole." R said," I feel you!" Carlos asked Richie," What was you doing in there?" Richie answered," I was in honor block my last year, every morning I did my calisthenics and took a birdbath in this little sink. After the count I went to college, I wanted to devote my time to reading and writing, with everything else secondary but I couldn't do that in prison. You have to keep your eyes open at all times or you won't make it. There is always some madness going on. The system is heinous, it got a lot of brothers stuck in the PPP cycle: prison- parole-prison. That shit is vicious, it's a struggle to get out of that cycle. Mr. Gray helped me a lot, he sent me a lot of mind-expanding literature. Gave me a book of quotations from the world's greatest thinkers Marx, Christ, Malcolm X, Lenin, Mao and Morton. I read about philosophy, economics and religion. He opened a New World of reading for me, I couldn't sit there and let my mind deteriorate like some of those inmates. He also sent me a lot of books about sales presentations, networking opportunities and the power of positive thinking. They have these programs that are suppose to teach you trades and things, shit that you can use when you get out, but here's the deal!! They give you a certificate and they say you are now qualified to go out and get a job, but no one is going to honor these certificates. It's null and void. And they act like they're doing something for you, but in reality, all they're doing is keeping their classes full so they can create jobs for the people that teach the class. Shit is crazy they send you 10 hours away, many miles from your family. How is somebody going to visit you up there and they don't got no money. Is that shit designed to rehabilitate or is it designed to destroy the family structure. Prisons are big business, I read in the newspaper that there are currently 1 million people behind bars in the USA. This represents the highest per capita incarceration rate in the world. Prison is no longer just a place for law-breakers it is a place of big business and cheap labor. Good old America investing, phone companies invest in jails, charging the prisoners extraordinary rates to get in touch with their families and did you know Seaman's furniture being build there and the list of companies goes on and they are only paying the prisoners 30 cents a hour. Cheap, cheap labor! Ain't too much you can do in prison, but get your head together and plan what you're going to do once you get out, that's the only real thing that keeps you going, the thought of getting out. Anyway I am not going to get into that right now. Mr. Gray got a job for me at the center and I'm going to try to get into New York University and finish my education. Get a good job in a year or two you know." R said," that's good sun, I'm not trying to knock you, but fuck all that shit I'm getting mines the fast way!" Richie said," different strokes, for different folks." DS cut him short before he could go on and said," Richie we'll talk about that later, right now let's get drunk and fuck these hoes!" Richie said," I'm ready sun" took a drink then said," Carlos, DS y'all niggas held me down in there, you know my moms abandoned me years ago. Without y'all, L, Mr. Gray and Shakim's help I don't think I would have ever made it home. Wise from the other side of 10th street never made it he died in there and Free high went in with two and got life now. Crazy! Yeah where's Fat Boy, Shakim and L at?" Carlos said," they're at the hotel waiting for us." Richie said," Good I want to see them!" The car pulled in front of the hotel, they got out and went to the lobby to wait for the elevator. DS used the hotel phone to call upstairs, L answered," yo, what's up?" DS said," get them girls ready, I got two rooms 711 and 712. Tell them to stay in that room you and Shakim come in the hallway." R yelled," DS come on the elevator is here!" DS hung up, they all got in the elevator, and there was this couple in there looking at us like we didn't belong in this hotel. Carlos looked at them too and laughed to his self we still got a long way to go. The white couple got off on the fifth floor, Richie said," fuck them is there any more Moet left?" R said," Yeah we got 20 bottles in the room." Richie said," I'm not drinking that much!" and laughed. The elevator stopped on the seventh floor, they got out and walked to the right. L and Shakim were at the ice and soda machine, they both yelled," oh shit Richie what's up?" Everyone gave each other hugs and pounds. L said," good to see you, it's been a long time word!" Shakim said," Word sun we missed your ass." They all started to reminiscence about old times, DS went in 711, he came back out a few minutes later, gave Rich some condoms and told him to go in. Betty and Chance were both dressed in exotic lingerie. Betty had a bottle of Moet in her hand, Chance had two glasses in her hands. Richie said," yeah!" and went in the room Chance took his arm and closed the door. They all clapped and went in room 712, DS opened another bottle and said," I know Richie is going to have a ball." Smiling R said," u know that, no pussy for 4 and half years, he's going crazy with them bitches right now." L turned the TV on, flicked thru all the stations trying to find something good to watch. He turned to the Jefferson's, they all found a place to sit down. L laughed at George doing that funny walk and yelling at Tom and Helen

Willis. R called DS and Carlos in the hallway and said," Los make sure you get the car on Sunday, it's on we got to take care of Tiny!" Carlos said," I'll get it don't worry about that." DS said," let's have fun tonight, we'll handle that shit" and went back in the room. 45 minutes later there was a knock on the door L opened the door Richie came in limping, with no shirt on, sweat was pouring off of him. He said," good looking sun" and went to lay on the bed "damn that felt good, them chicks are official freaks." L said," hell yeah!" R and DS went to the other room, Carlos asked Richie," where are you going to stay at?"

He said," with my uncle in flushing just until I get on my feet." Carlos said," cool here's my cell number call me tomorrow, so we can go shopping. I know u need some gear!" Richie said," Word! I don't have anything." Carlos's beeper went off, he went to the phone it was Tracey. She answered on the first ring," hello." Carlos said," What's up baby, how was the burial?" She said," it was very upsetting, Mrs. Davis was trying to hold on, but Tonya was going crazy she passed out I had to help her back to the limo." Carlos said," Damn! That's fucked up, am I going to see you today." She said," yes, where r u at?" He said," in flushing, we went to pick up my man Richie he just came home." She said," okay call me when you're finished, I'm going to get into my books, so it maybe better if we get together tomorrow."

Carlos smiled to himself and said," yeah that's a good idea, I'll see you after work." She said," alright bye and be safe." And they hung up. DS and R came back in the room, DS asked Richie," are you ready for round two?" Richie put his hand up, DS grabbed and pulled him off the bed, he almost fell over pulling Richie up. DS said," damn kid you're a heavy motherfucker!" Richie went back to the other room, when he came out this time he said," DS take me home I'm drained sun." Everybody started laughing DS said," okay!" DS called the car back, everybody left and the driver took them to Astoria first to drop Betty and Chance off, and then they went to the hood. DS paid the driver, everybody gave Richie pounds and hugs. DS and Richie got in the BMW and pulled off. L, Shakim, R, and Carlos all exchanged pounds, Carlos went to his mother's house to get some rest.

Chapter 17

The next day R called Carlos," Los go get that car everything is set up." He said," okay I'll call you from Brooklyn we can meet out there." R said," okay call me as soon as you get there." Carlos said," cool, peace." He went to shower and change after he got out his mother and him talked for a while. She asked him about Chip's wake, he was telling her about it and the phone rang. Carlos went to answer it, it was Head," Los what's up are you going to work tonight?" Carlos said," Nah sun I'm going to lay up tonight, going to my aunt's house it's a family thing." He said," alright but come see me when you get back." Carlos said," I'll call as soon as I get back." He said," Peace." And they hung up, He went and gave his mother a kiss and told her," He'll be back later." She said," be safe and make sure you call." He said," okay!" He went to 40th Ave and 12th street to call a cab, 10 minutes later the car came. He got in the cab, told the driver to take me to Brooklyn, Evergreen and Dekalb Ave. When he got there he paid the driver and walked up the block to his cousin Tony's house. Tony was standing out front with a few friends, Carlos gave him a pound and said," Tony did you get the car for me?" Tony said," Yeah, come around the back" he told his homeboys he'd see them later. They walked around the corner there was this new jet black Audi 5000. He said," that's the car I got for you, just took it like a hour ago from Queens so it shouldn't be that hot yet." Carlos said," good let me use the phone in the house." They went back to Tony's house, Carlos went to the living room to beep DS. Then to the kitchen to get something to drink. Tony's wife was at the table eating with their son, Carlos went and gave her a kiss and hug. Asked her," how are things going?" She said," everything is fine, Tony should of told me you was coming I would of cooked more food." Carlos said," thank you but I'm alright, next time." Tony called him to the phone it was DS. Carlos said to him," I'm in Brooklyn at Tony's house I got the car I'm just waiting for y'all to come." DS said," We're on our way now, so just lay for us." Carlos said," okay I'll be here." Tony and Carlos went out front and were playing basketball on his homemade hoop. Tony won the first game of 21, by 6 points, they was half way thru the second game, DS pulls up with R and L. They got out and they all walked to where Tony parked the Audi. R said," yeah this will do." Tony," I told you Los, I wouldn't let u down." They all walked back to Tony's house but this time he took them in by the upstairs door. DS went to his car and came upstairs with a black duffel bag. They all went to Tony's room and sat down, DS opened the bag and gave everyone a Glock and some black gloves. DS said," I wiped down all of the guns and the bullets so we don't leave no prints, don't take the gloves off until we're home safe." R, L and Carlos went and got in the

Audi, L was driving they parked on Tiny's block four houses away, he had to drive past them because the block was a one way.

Tiny lived in the Fort Greene part of Brooklyn by City Tech College. There were a lot of nice houses in this neighborhood. They waited for a few hours, final Tiny's brown Jeep drove by, they slid down. He didn't see them, his mind was occupied with thoughts of fucking Gloria. When he parked in his driveway Gloria unzipped his pants and started jerking his dick, he closed his eyes and told her," come on baby suck it baby." He leaned back, R and Carlos walked to the jeep, R went to the driver's side, and Carlos went to passenger side. With the but of the gun he broke the window, Tiny opened his eyes shocked and surprised, he pushed Gloria off of him and tried to reach under his sit. It was too late Carlos fired the first bullet stuck him in the chest, he grabbed his chest and fell back. R then shot him twice in the head, blood and brains flew all over the place. L drove up, Gloria got out of the jeep, they all jumped in the Audi and drove off. Carlos hands were shaking and butterflies were in his stomach, Gloria, R and Carlos got out on Tony's block, L drove off in the car. DS and Tony were sitting on DS's car. DS said," Los is everything alright, you look pale as a ghost." Carlos said," I'm okay let's just get the fuck out of here." DS, Gloria and R got in the car.

Carlos gave his cousin $3,000 dollars and told him," thanks L is going to dump that car, I'll call you tomorrow so you can come to my hood." They gave one another pounds and Carlos got in the car and they drove off back to Q.B. DS parked by the 24-hour store, Carlos went in to get some beers. R and Gloria walked in the block to his crib. DS and Carlos went and sat on the benches by 21 street and started talking. DS said," Carlos you didn't look so good back there are you okay." Carlos said," nah it's nothing I was just a little nervous but I'm good now and took a drink of beer.

DS said," one down and one more to go, after we take care of Head this whole shit is going to be ours!" Carlos said," word lets make a move on him ASAP." DS said," I got that mapped out, you know he always be going to Studio 54, we're going to hit him up there, so it doesn't look funny and make the hood hot." Carlos said," cool just let me know when! I'm going to see Tracey see you later."

Chapter 18

Carlos gave him a pound and went to see if Tracey was still out here at Tisha's house. Carlos walked to Tisha's building the lobby door was locked, so he started to call Tracey out the window. No one was answering, this man came out the building Carlos ran and caught the door before it closed. He then walked upstairs to Tisha's crib, he could hear an Al B Sure song blasting from her apartment, and he banged on the door. Tisha opened it, she said," don't be banging on my door like that!" He said," I was calling you from down stairs the music was to loud that's why I knocked like that." She said," Come in." Tracey was sitting on the carpet looking at Tisha's CD collection. She got up, went to the table and poured herself a drink of Hennessy on the rocks. She asked me," Do u want anything to drink?" He said," nah I was drinking some beers already." They went and sat on the sofa, she asked," where was you at today?" Carlos said," at my aunt's house fixing her table, don't you have to go to school tomorrow?" She said," no it's a holiday tomorrow some Jewish thing." He said," okay I didn't know that, let's go out tonight?" She said," okay let me get ready." He said," I'll meet you down stairs." She said," I'll be there in a few." Carlos got up to leave but first he said bye to Tisha, she was at the table playing solitaire. Tisha said," Carlos don't play with my cousin's feeling, I'm hoping you are serious about this." He told her," I'm very real about her, I wouldn't do anything to hurt her." She said," I'm going to take you're word, don't make me bust your ass about this" and smiled. He said," come on 'Tis chill with that" and playfully grabbed her. She said," alright Carlos don't play."

He went out the door and down the stairs to wait for her. Troy and Ebony walked by, Carlos called for them to come here. Troy gave him a pound and said," what's up sun?" Carlos said," ain't shit about to go to the city with Tracey." Ebony said," Damn nigga I didn't see you in a while what's up? You ain't fucking with me no more?" he could sense a hint of jealousy in her tone. Carlos said," knock that off Ebony you know you're my peoples for life." She said," call me when you get the time." He said," I'm going to do that word." Troy said," Yo, sun I was at the store and that bitch Sarah was in there talking to Leeza telling her that Tiny got murdered in Brooklyn at his crib." Carlos looked shocked and said," Word, when did that happened?" Troy said," I really don't know if it's true or not, I'm just letting u know what she said." Carlos said," Anyway who gives a fuck I don't." Ebony said," word fuck that nigga, it's good for him if it did happen." Tracey came out the building, she walked over to them. She spoke to Troy and Ebony and asked Carlos was he ready? He gave Troy a pound and told Ebony," he would call her."

Tracey and Carlos walked to 21 street to get a cab to the city. They took the cab to 59th street and fifth Ave, they got out and walked into Central Park. They walked to the little pond in the park, Carlos picked up some rocks and threw them in the water. She asked," Carlos what do you want in life?" He said," I just want to be successful and happy." She said," how are you going to do that selling drugs, having to always look over your back and always on the run?" He said," that is just a stepping stone to get what I want." She said," What do you want?" He said," a store or business I could run and just lay back." She said," that's cool at least you got some ideas, just always remember those ideas and work towards them. Plan your work and work that plan" Carlos said," I'm going to try." They walked to this little diner on fifth Ave to eat, after they ate he paid the bill and they went to get a cab back to Queens.

They drove pass the 41 side of Vernon, the block was taped off. Carlos said," damn something is always happening out here." They got out the cab on 40 Ave and 12th street. They got out and he asked her," are you coming to my sister's house with me?" She said," I don't think I should do that, I'm a little tipsy and don't want to do something I'll regret later." he told her," just come on I really want to be with you tonight." She looked in his eyes, kissed him and grabbed his hand. They walked across the street to his sister's block and went upstairs. Everybody was asleep in the apartment, he unlocked his bedroom and they went in. Tracey kissed with passion, he led her to the bed. They slowly undressed. Softly he kissed her exposed breast, she moaned he positioned him self on top off her. He was inside her stroking slowly, then fast she put her arms around him. She moved her body so he was deep inside her, their bodies moved in a perfect rhythm. She tightened her grip, her body moved in short jerking moves, they both came at the same time. He laid on the side of her, she put her head on his chest and they both fell asleep.

Later that night they went at it again, after they was done they just laid there talking. The next morning he took her home, he told her to call him and kissed and hugged her. She went in the house and he went back to the hood, to his mother's house to shower and change. His mother was on the phone when he walked in the door, she said," I tried to beep you I was worried about you, I told you to call." He looked at his beeper the light was off, He said," no wonder why I didn't get any beeps the battery is dead. I'm sorry for not calling. I was at Nelly's house." She said," I called there the ringer must have been off, if you go back over there tell her to call me." He said," I'll go tell her." She said," DS been calling here all day and some girl named Donna. Wait a minute I got her number." She went by the phone and gave me a paper with her number on it. He looked at the paper and put it in his pocket. He said," mommy I'm going out, I'll make sure I call you if I'm going to stay out." She said," please call I was up all night worried." She got her pocketbook, took out a few 20 dollar bills and handed them to him. She said," give that to Jason I don't want to know where he's at, but tell him I love him and to be safe." He looked at her and said," Okay" and left out the door.

Chapter 19

After Tiny's funeral and burial Prinz and Ant-Wop was walking Tiny's wife to the car, Prinz opened the back door and let April in. Tiny's wife was distraught and grieving hard. Tiny was her life, he did everything for her, and she was feeling like her life was lost without him. Prinz closed the door behind her. Ant-wop got in the back seat to be next to her. Prinz went and got in the driver's seat to drive April home. Ant-wop said to her" everything is going to be alright April, you got to be strong for them babies, you know sun always taught you 2 be strong" April weakly replied" I know but it's just hard" tears streaming down her face. Prinz started to drive off, April was so much in a daze she didn't realize Prinz was driving in the wrong direction from her house. When April realized she said" where are you going?' that's when Ant-wop pulled out the 357 magnum on her. Ant-wop said" shut the fucking up bitch before you join your husband and never see the light of day again!" April reached for the rear door handles but they wouldn't open. Prinz just busted out laughing. April tried to swing on Ant-wop before she got the chance he slapped her in the face with the magnum. Ant-wop said" didn't I tell you to be silent bitch" then he put his hand over her mouth. Prinz pulled in this garage where two other cars awaited. The garage door closed it was dimly lighted in there. R got out the car smiling.

R, Prinz and Ant-wop had this planned for a long time. Prinz and Wop was from Brownsville, they once worked in one of Tiny's spots out there. Prinz and R met on Rikers Island where Prinz was being held on a $10,000 bail that Tiny left him in jail on. Prinz was bitter towards Tiny. Prinz, Antwop and R were in mod9 in c74 on the island together. Once Prinz and R found out they had similar enemies that's where their bond started. R hatched the plan and Prinz followed it to the letter. R was true to his word, once he got his case dismissed he bailed Prinz out and they got started on the Tiny plan.

Chapter 20

When Carlos got outside the sun was glisten it was going to be a nice day. He walked to the corner store to get the newspaper and some Newport's. Brother Al was on the corner handing out pamphlets, Carlos tried to walk pass, but he ran up to him and said," here little brother take one, the Lord loves us all." Carlos took it from him and was looking at it as he was going back to his block. DS walked up behind him and took the pamphlet out of his hand. DS said," Carlos what's up? Why did you take that shit from him, it's a whole bunch of bullshit! Brother Al got some act going on, as many people he put in the dirt. Now he's on some church shit acting like he got a halo on his head. Him and the Rev. at that church are the biggest hypocrites I know." Carlos said," Why do you say that?" DS said," don't you know that the Rev. is fucking all of the girls in the church, taking all the old ladies money, not giving nothing back. Driving around in a newer BMW then mines. Brother Al is a different story that motherfucker there will kill anybody for a few dollars. He's on Blue's payroll, if Blue tells him to take care of somebody I bet you we wouldn't see whoever no more." Carlos said," people are funny in the hood, it seems like everybody got some funny shit going on. Sun on the reels don't be grabbing nothing out my hand like that." He then grabbed

him and they started wrestling, after a few rounds they stopped.
DS said," alright sun stop playing." They both laughed, they walked in 10th street and sat on the bench. DS said," be ready this weekend we're going to Studio 54." Carlos said," cool I'm going to try to get Tracey to go to my aunt's house for a few days. I'll come back on Saturday." DS," all right we got all the work we need, but if Head finds out we're doing our thing, you know the beef will start here. Let's get him out the way then it's on." Carlos said," Cool my nigga." Then gave him a pound and went back to my mother's house.

Carlos called Tracey, she answered," Hello." he said," what's up baby?" Tracey," hey what's up Carlos?" He said," I was thinking about you so I called to see what you was doing." She said," nothing I was reading one of my text books, trying to stay ahead." He said," that's good I was wondering if you would like to come upstate with me to my aunt's house for a few days. I know you got school this week and work this weekend, but see if you can get off." She said," I haven't missed a day, I think I should be able to do it, call me back later, I have to make a few phone calls." Carlos said," after you're done just call me at my mother's house." His mother was getting dinner ready. He went and sat on the sofa, turned on the TV and was flicking thru the channels. His mother came and sat besides him, they started chatting about life. She said," Carlos I'm so tried of living here, after the incident that happened with Jason I'm uncomfortable." Carlos said," I understand, I'm going to try to get us out of here." She said," I know you're going too." And went back to the oven to check on her food. He got up and went to the back room to call Tracey. She said," I was about to call you, I'm going with you what time are we leaving?" He said," as soon as you're ready, just come to my mother's house." She said," okay I'm going to get my things ready, be there soon." He went to get a few things for the trip and laid down until she came.

He called the bus station to get the time schedule of the buses that were going to Danbury, CT. He made sure the 8 p.m. bus wasn't sold out, Tracey called, he told her to meet him at 6 so they could go. They met at 6 and got in a cab to the bus station, the ride to get there was three hours. His aunt met them at the bus station and took them to her house. Her house was nice, three floors, five bedrooms and three bathrooms, she let them sleep in the guestroom. The weather was nice so they went out to the patio to sit and have a few drinks. His aunt and her husband Bruce joined them, his aunt Sharon moved here six years ago. She worked in the college here, she been trying to get him to move up here and attend the school. He was to busy thinking about the hustle, then to go to school and to leave the city, hell no it was nice to visit but to live he thought not. The days there went by fast. Later that day Sharon took them horseback riding. The next day they chartered a boat to go fishing. Carlos nor Bruce didn't catch anything, but Tracey and Sharon caught four fish and it was Tracey's first time fishing. Sharon cleaned and cooked the fish that night for dinner. Carlos and his Aunt Sharon were in the kitchen talking while she was setting the table for dinner. She said," the reason I moved here was to make a better life for my kids and me. The schools have better teachers. Did you know that inner city schools have the lowest citywide exams. The reason for this is all of the teachers with the highest grade point averages get to teach at the school of their choice, so you know their not picking inner cities schools.

Of course no one, who goes to school for 4 to 10 years want to deal with bad neighborhood, kids. It's very rare and unique when you find a teacher that doesn't care about the paycheck but has a passion to teach the lil ones. I know that teachers are underpaid, so when people say money doesn't matter, they're rich or lying. The better the place you live the more chance you have to give your child a fair shot at better schooling and a safer environment. The whole system is screwed up, it's just not fair."

Tracey and Carlos took the bus early that morning, Sharon took them back to the bus station. Sharon said," make sure y'all come back soon to visit." Tracey said," we will thank you so much, I'm going to drag his but up here real soon." Sharon laughed and gave them both a hug and kiss good-bye. The ride home seemed faster then the ride there, Tracey slept the whole ride back. When they got back Carlos asked," did you enjoy yourself?" She said," Yes I did when are we going back?" Carlos said," soon" He got our bags from under the bus and flagged down a cab to take us back to Queens. He dropped her off at her house first, and then went to the hood. He took his bags to his sister's house, took a shower and a nap.

Chapter 21

When he got up Carlos put on his black guess pants, black wallabies and a blue shirt. Carlos went to Shakim's grandmother's house cause that's where Shakim had stayed. Shakim answered the door, Carlos said," Shakim what's up kid? We exchanged pounds, he said," ain't nothing this computer-programming course in kicking my ass. I'm ready to quit!" Carlos looked at him shocked and said," what, are you crazy nigga. You came too far to loose focus. You're the most positive nigga with us. Don't go out like that!" He said," Los you don't know it's just hard sometimes." Carlos said," I can only imagine! I know it's a struggle but the reward of your struggle is going to be great. Sun you know that." Shakim," true I love computers it's just the schedule, I can't hang out like I use to." Carlos said," you ain't missing shit. This shit out here is still going to be here sun, I don't want to hear no shit like that again. Keep at it!" Carlos gave him a few thousand dollars and said," call L, DS, R or me if you ever need anything you hear me." Shakim said," I'm not going to quit, I just be stressed out sometimes you know." Carlos said," now that's the Sha I know." Then they walked to the hill to see who was up there.

Carlos saw Stacey coming out of the supermarket, he walked over to her. Her arm was in a sling and cast, she was moving slowly. Lisa was with her carrying the bags, Carlos pulled Stacey to the side and said," how are you doing? Is everything okay?" She said," I'm doing better, thank you for sending Kiesha up to the hospital to make sure my TV and phone stayed on." Carlos said," come on now that was the least I could do." She said," the police was trying to pressure me to tell on your brother, but I kept telling them that it's wasn't him or Cash." Carlos said," that was real, thanks! I'm sorry about what happened." She said," I grew up with Jewel and I know he wouldn't do anything to hurt me. People out here are awful, a lot of people you think is cool were telling me to tell on him. But fuck that I know he didn't mean to do this to me." Carlos gave her a hug and told her," I'll be by the crib later to hit you off." She said," alright." Then her and Lisa went down the hill.

DS and Richie pulled up, the music was blasting from his car he double-parked and got out. He gave Carlos and Shakim a pound then said," what's the deal? Los how was the trip, did you tell Sharon I said hello?" Carlos said," yeah I told her, it was nice I was bugging up there! What was going on out here?" DS," yo, you missed it Troy was drunk and bugging, he beat the shit out of that chick Monica. That shit was funny she was trying to fight back but sun was killing her. He was going to far, he was about to kick her in the face but I stopped him. He didn't know who I was because I grabbed him from behind. He was like you better get off of me whoever this is before I start whipping your ass. When I told him it was me he chilled out. Carlos said," that nigga is still crazy." They all laughed. DS," he's lucky I talked Monica out of going to the police, he better chill with that shit." Richie," word, he needs to chill, but we all know Troy he's never going to change for nobody." Shakim," that's just how he is!" Carlos said," true!"

Richie," yo, you know that Poppy got hit at the parole board with 18 months, this dude I was with wrote me and told me." DS," word" and started to laugh. Richie," that shit isn't funny kid, you know how that shit is stress!" Carlos said," I know that's fucked up." DS," Rich and Sha, me and Los got some biz to handle, we'll see y'all later." We gave Rich and Sha pounds and got in DS's car. DS said" fuck that dude Pop by time he gets out we will be sleeping on money and driving brand new BMWs ."

Chapter 22

DS drove to the Ave, parked and they went to R's house. Once they got there, he beeped L.

R," are y'all ready?" Carlos said," of course nigga are you ready?" R," born ready kid." They went to the back room, him and Gloria started to yell at each other in Spanish. The phone rang DS answered it," speak about it. Yeah come to R's house we're waiting for you." And hung up. R slammed the room door and came out with an over night bag and sat on the sofa beside them. R," that bitch drives me crazy sometimes!"

They waited for L to come, a little while later L knocked on the door he had a bottle of vodka in one hand a blunt in the other. L," what's up everybody? Yo, R is there any orange juice?" R said," Yeah go ahead in the kitchen." L came back with three glasses, handed Carlos and R one. They all poured their own drinks, they sat around and got high to 11:30 that night, and then DS went to get the car. They got in and headed to Manhattan, DS pulled over and parked on 55th street around the corner from the club. R went in the bag and gave them all infa-red glocks. The line to get in the club was long, DS called Dan the security guard at the club, Dan lived in their hood too. Dan told DS and them to go to the side entrance in order for them to avoid the line and the metal-detectors. R gave Dan a hand full of bills, Dan said," good-looking, y'all enjoy yourselves. It was after midnight but the nightclub was very crowded. At one end people were dancing, the lights were flashing in and out. Carlos noticed Head posted at the bar buying $250 bottles of Cristal champagne. He had four ladies dancing around him. They went in the bathroom to get ready for the attack. R and DS walked up behind Head pulled the guns out and started to fire. They hit Head seven times point-blank range, he fell over a wave of confusion broke out everyone was running towards the exits. L and Carlos ran towards the doors they came in. They both pulled out when they seen Dan and fired, he fell down as they ran past, L stopped over him and fired three more shots to make sure he was dead. He was the only real witness that knew them, They put the guns away before they went out the exit door. Tony pulled up, they got in the car and speeded away. They could hear the cop's car sirens blaring, but it was too late they were gone.

Chapter 23

A year later R, L, Gloria, DS, Maria and Carlos was at the bag up house they had in Corona. R was in the kitchen mixing the cocaine and baking soda together. He had twenty 50-gram pieces of crack already cooked. They was there all day, R already cooked the first five kilos they had now he was on the last. Gloria and Maria were at the table in the living room, bagging up grams of cocaine power. Everything has been good for them since they took care of Head and Tiny, they had the whole hood to work on now. They had a team of 40 workers that sold everything crack, grams of powder, weed and dope for them. They was selling a lot of work, the Dominican connect R hooked them up with loved them. L brought a new red Volvo, R had a new gray Jaguar and Carlos had a Cadillac. They all tried to stay low because the hood was full of jealous niggers that would get you trapped.

Shakim was almost done with his computer classes, Mr. Gray got him an internship at IBM, he was chilling. DS gave him the BMW he had because he coped a newer model. Richie was teaching at York College making good for himself. DS said," R I'm about to go back to the hood, me and Wanda are going to the flicks." R said," Go ahead we got this!" DS gave them all pounds and left out the door,

Gloria went and locked the door. Carlos went and sat on the couch with L, he was sitting their watching porno tapes. Carlos said," damn sun that's all you watch when we're here, turn that shit off." L," come on nigga look at that bitch she's getting busy." He started laughing. Carlos's portable phone rang, it was Tracey, she said," Carlos come to Queensbrige now, I got some bad news to tell you!" he could hear it in her voice that something was terribly wrong. He said," what's wrong baby?" She said," just come out here, I don't want to tell you on the phone." His thoughts was racing he didn't know what was going on. She just started to cry and said," just come right now." He was bugging, He ran in the kitchen, grabbed his car keys and was about to run out the door. L jumped off the sofa and said," Los what the fuck is wrong?" Carlos said," I don't know Tracey called me crying telling me to come out there, but she wouldn't tell me why." L," I'm going with you hold on." Carlos said," Hurry up!" They got in his car, drove down Northern Blvd to 38th Ave to 21 street. Once they got there it was hectic. 12th and 40 avenue was barracked with the yellow crime scene tape. They knew when they seen that to expect the worse, but they wouldn't have never in a million years expect what happened that day.

L and Carlos parked the car and walked towards the block, once they got there Ms Pat and a few others was standing they're grieving. Tracey came out of the building pass the police barrack's. She came over and hugged Carlos. She was, crying, Carlos kept asking her what was wrong. The anticipation of what lied ahead was tremendous. He had to tell her to calm down and stop crying so she could tell him what was going on. Before she could get the words out, Ms Pat said," the police was trying to arrest Richie for trespassing in his own building, so he started to argue with them, they started hitting him so he started to defend himself, he was trying to tell them he couldn't breathe. You know that cocksucker Rambo didn't listen to him, I went to the precinct to see if he was okay because when they were bringing him out of the building it looked like he wasn't moving. Once Tracey and me got there they told us that he was taking to the hospital for a possible drug overdose. They went to Astoria General. They wouldn't tell us nothing until Tracey saw Ray. (Ray works at the hospital doing x-rays) Ray told us the police brought him in DOA, the cops were saying he was on drugs, the doctors tried to bring him back but couldn't. We know he wasn't on drugs, they fucking killed him in that holding cell!" Carlos was in total shock, he couldn't believe what he just heard. It was like everything was going in slow motion, Shawn walked by them and threw a bottle at one of the police cars, that's all it took for people to start going crazy. People were going nuts, breaking car windows, screaming, one dude started flipping the trash cans over and then he set them on fire. It was like the 60's watts riots, firemen was trying to put out fires that were set, but they couldn't cause people were throwing rocks, bottles and all types of shit off of the roofs.

Tracey, L and Carlos walked to Karen's crib, Carlos was still in a daze, he couldn't believe Richie was dead. At the moment he started thinking of all the things he wanted to tell him and now never could. He was doing great, got a crib, enrolled in law school and was helping Mr. Gray with the kids. He started to mess with Karen this older lady and fell in love. All his time was used towards positive situations since he came out of jail. It's funny and sad that the righteous ones always seem to get taken first. Karen was sitting at her table crying uncontrollably. Carlos embraced her as much as he could while trying to hold in the tears that flowed down his face. There was nothing he could say or do, the loss of Richie took a huge toll on all of them in the community.

After they buried Richie, Mr. Gray and the Reverend Chase held a meeting at the community center. The place was full of people of all ages and colors, students from his school, teachers and a few new reporters from all channels. Mr. Gray took the podium first, he cleared his voice, and you could hear the sorrow and pain from within. Mr. Gray said," this whole thing gives me a sour taste in my mouth. This is a tremendous wrongdoing, how can we let this killer cop get away with this?" The crowd applauded but he continued," I spoke to the captain of the 114th precinct, all they did was suspend officer Longley, until the grand jury decision is brought fourth. How absurd is that, we know Richie didn't do drugs! Officer Longley must face the consequences. His discrimination and brutal act took Richie Travels life! They treated him like a common thug, since he was arrested before, they act like they did no wrongdoings. This whole community knows of officer Longley's notorious ways of handling things. So many people put in various civilian complains about him, more than any other cop in the 114th precinct. A total of fifteen complaints were filed against him during a six -month span. Only about 15% of the city's cops get even a single complaint over a course of a year, but still they did nothing, and are still doing nothing after he took a promising black man's life. They're lack of discipline given to the New York Police Department's officers allowed this to happen. We aren't going to leave City Hall on broken promises and neglect this type of violence, we will not have it continue.

Most of the victims that these kind of incidents happen to are young, black and Spanish men. These men are dying in forgotten neighborhoods under the hands of the NYPD, but we will not rest until justice is done. It is vital for our young men to learn early on how to handle themselves when confronted and put in these type of situations. We all must defend ourselves against killer cops. They were acting like this murder was within the departmental guidelines. All the information describing what happened was being filtered by the police. I asked them what did happened, they said officer Longley and his colleagues did nothing wrong. But what happened was that individuals with a shield on their chest, choked and beat and took the life of a young man, they murdered him. If they took their badges off and did it, they would be prosecuted for murder and that's exactly what this was MURDER!! This was modern day madness, the police are out of control. We have to be committed to guaranteeing that justice will be served for Richie Travels and for embattled young men not only in Queensbridge but all over the United States. As we express our sympathy, we also are speaking out to assure that there is a strong unwavering voice for the voiceless everywhere. Clearing his voice Mr. Gray went on," we are a people that are in trouble and until we become a people that make them respect us as the human beings we are born to be, it is always going to be this madness. I'm out here not just to make the police realize that they're wrong for what they did to Mr. Travels, I'm here to tell my people that we're wrong for not making them understand that as a people, we will not tolerate it. Which means we will not do things to ourselves that make us seem weak, we will not destroy us and we not sit back and let them destroy us. Richie Travels made a big change from a boy to a man. He was working hard to prove that statistic that claims 80% of people who are released from prison will end up back in prison wrong. It seems like these people always take the individual that is trying to walk a straight path away from us, but for his sake and honor we'll have to keep fighting to make sure this doesn't happened again.

I've been in the streets, I know the outcome. We're losing the youth, I don't have to be here helping I made it out, but I refuse to forget my struggles, that's why I'm here to show the youth they can make it out too. Richie was a big part of me showing them, he was the perfect product. He was not just talking the talk, Richie was doing his part. He didn't have to come to the community center everyday after work and school to help the kids in this projects, he did it because he was about change, he believed it in his heart. He wanted to show them there was another way and he knew education was a great tool in achieving it. He spent countless hours instilling that in the youth out here. He knew from small beginnings comes great things. Richie Travels knew that no matter who you are and how determined your drive, your road to success was paved by others. A teacher, a parent, a mentor, somebody gave you the jewels to move forward. Richie was all of these things to these kids and to people in this community and to have him taken from us like this is a great, great lost. I was proud of his growth as a man. He once said to me at some point the pupil got to be the teacher. That statement was so poignant, because eventually he taught me a few things. I am a living testament to his strength and his influence to these kids. We most all know that True power is in unity and knowledge. He would want us to know that! Thank you as he walked off, the audience went crazy. Carlos looked around older men and women were yelling. Carlos thought back trying to imagine their lives being older and black they seen a whole lot of this type of shit in their days.

The deacon took the mic," thank you Mr. Gray." More applauds," I encourage every one to come out with us peacefully to rally and March to that precinct and demand answers." He motioned for everyone to go to the tables to get food and drinks. After that a few people got up and spoke of Richie, but the most profound speaker was Mr. Gray we'll always remember everything he said. When it first happened it was on the second page of the Daily News, but as time went by the less you heard of it, like the majority of the incidents that affect black people, soon after nothing is spoken of it again.

Chapter 24

Pop has been locked up for five and a half years now, he was now placed in the Otisville Correctional facility. Otisville is a nondescript stretch of land similar to a college however when you see the huge gun towers and barbed wires fences snaking around the top you knew it wasn't a college.

The officers at the check in desk make Zora take off her shoes, belt, and empty her pockets, the only thing that was allowed in was the quarters for the vendor machines. Zora walked into a drag looking cafeteria in which several inmates in green uniforms were sitting with their visitors, side by side at uncomfortably low tables (so nothing could be passed underneath) playing cards, checkers and simply talking. The inmates are of all varieties, corn rowed youngins looking no older than 20, elderly figures who seem familiar from a hundred prison movies. Pop comes in garrulous greets the fellow inmates, then gives Zora a hug and kiss and sits down. Pop" good to see u big cousin, how's the rest of the family?" Zora says" things aren't that good Head got killed at some club in the city." Pop" why the fuck didn't Aunt Terri tell me? , I just spoke to her the other day!" He was furious, Zora" I told her not to that's why I came up here myself to tell you. I don't want you to do anything in here to stop you from coming home, we need you home." Tears were running down Pop's face he just put his head in Zora's lap.

Inmates are bunched up, whites, blacks and Spanish all packed together in small groups, the warden didn't allow a group of more than five to be assembled, for the fear of a riot. By the weight bench Pop got up breathing heavy, he was a slim built, dark skinned brother, who had his hair in cornrows. In his eyes you could see the evil, Pop did some very unspeakable things in his life. His comrade Buck got under the 250lbs. weight bar and Pop went to the back of the bench to spot him. Buck said," Pop I heard Carlos, DS, L, and some dude R is blowing up out there." Pop said," yeah I been hearing the same shit too, I got a plan for them dudes when I get out of here." Buck said," you know I'm with u hopefully we'll make the parole board this month." Pop let out a high pitch laugh," all hell is going to break loose, when I get out of here, the word on the streets is they all had something to do with my cousin Head getting hit at that club.

If I make this board, you'll see how I handle things, now stop bullshitting and do your set." Pop put his hand on top of the bar and Buck pushed up the weight, took a deep breath and started his work out.

Chapter 25

It was very hot, the degrees was 90, it felt like the inside of an oven. On the block the sprinkler was on, (the ghetto pool) all the kids and some adults was having water fights with water balloons, guns and buckets to stay cool. Shakim grabbed a bucket full of water from one of the kids and hid behind a tree. DS and Carlos were standing there looking as L walked in the block. He had on some sky-blue Ballys, guess shorts and a sky-blue North Carolina jersey. He walked over to them and gave them a pound. L said," what's up? What are y'all doing today? I was thinking about going to the beach with Sarah and wanted to see if y'all was going to roll." DS said," I don't know yet, it's too hot to go to the beach, its no shade there." They both stood there watching as Shakim ran behind L with a bucket of ice cold water raised, he poured the whole bucket over L's head. It reminded Carlos of when a basketball team wins a game and the team soaks the coach. L jumped up, getting his wind back, he was pissed off. L said," Shakim you stupid motherfucker, what the fuck is wrong with you!" They all laughed at him, he didn't find it funny at all. L," u fucked up my $200 dollars shoes and now my beeper is wet." Shakim," damn my bad, you don't have to get so upset it's just water!" L," fuck that!" then stormed off the block. Shakim ran back over to the kids and started playing water games with them.

DS said," yo L was madder than a motherfucker that got cut off of welfare!" They both laughed, R walked up.

R," what's the deal kid?" They all gave each other pounds. R said," what's so funny?" DS repeated to him what just happened. R started laughing too and said," I was looking for y'all I was going to call but I figured y'all was on the block so I walked over here." DS said," yeah we were just chilling." R said," that dude Fella been coming short a lot on the packs I been giving him lately." Carlos said," how short and what the fuck is wrong with him?" R said," at first it was just a few hundred, I let it go, but now it's like five grand. I been looking for him, but nobody has seen him around." DS said," five grand?" R said," yeah! Let's go get right and see if we can find this dude." Carlos said," If he's not out here, he's most likely in Astoria." R said," Ebony told me, he's getting high, smoking crack joints." DS said," word not that nigga!" Carlos said," he might be you never know, that's why he's coming up short all the fucking time." R said," I'm going to get the van, meet me by the 24 hour store."

As he walked to get in the van, DS and Carlos went to the 24-hour store. R pulled up a few minutes later, DS and Carlos got in the van, R hit a switch and the side panel of the van opened, there was two nines in there. DS and Carlos each took one, they got to Astoria, R double parked on 8th street. They walked to Fella's aunt's house, once they got in the building they could hear infants crying and small children shouting, the babble of several TV sets and jazz, hip-hop, and salsa music leaking though the thin walls.

They knocked on the door, Fella's aunt Nikki answered the door. She said," what's up DS come in." Once they got inside her baby was sleeping on the floor on a cushion from the sofa, but there wasn't a sofa in her house. Looking around at the pictures on her wall, Carlos saw photos of her in her younger days, also photos of her older son, from junior high school along with a photo of him in a football uniform holding a helmet. Also there were a few photos of a happy family, before her drug use tore it apart. DS asked Nikki," is Fella here?" Nikki said," yeah he asleep in the backroom, go ahead and wake him up. DS y'all got the best product around here, can I get a few pieces?" DS threw her two grams of cook up, she knew what was going on but she didn't care as long as she got to smoke that demon. DS went to the backroom to wake Fella up, he was sleeping on the floor, rolled up between two sheets. DS kicked him in his back, Fella screamed and rolled over. Fella," yo, what did u do that for!" DS," get the fuck up nigga" and pulled out the gun, " you're lucky I didn't just shoot your dumb ass." Fella," come on D please don't do me like this." Begging. DS," put on your fucking shoes, we're going for a walk." Fella was fumbling around for his shoes saying," yo man we can talk here, we don't have to go outside. Fella's clothes were all dirty like he didn't change them in a few days. DS hit him across the bridge of his nose, he screamed in pain, blood was pouring out of his nose. Nikki heard the scream, put down her pipe and tried to get up. R pulled out his gun and told her," if you fucking move I'm going to blow your head off, you know what this is about, it was cool when you helped him smoke my shit up!" DS pistol whipped Fella a few more times, Fella was yelling," I'm sorry D I'll do anything, please give me a chance." DS said," go wash the fuck up and come on." He walked Fella to the bathroom, Fella got a towel and cleaned up as much as possible. They came to the front of the crib, Fella looking like a scared puppy knowing he would be next to be put to sleep, when he seen R the worse the look got. R said," Fella don't worry, I'm not going to kill your ass this time, you got a lot of free work to do, but I promise you the next time. you're dead!" Fella said," ok R I know, you don't have to worry there's never going to be a next time."

They all walked back to the van and started to drive back to the hood. R was seated next to Fella, DS was driving and Carlos was in the passenger seat. Carlos turned to Fella and asked," what the fuck is wrong with you, how did you start messing with that shit?" Fella looked up at him and said," I messed up, I was fucking with Kenya and she got me to try it once and after I did there was no turning back. I made the biggest mistake of my life." Carlos said," that's crazy Fella, you know first hand not to fuck with that, you seen it destroy your aunt's family." R said," I don't give a fuck who started him fucking with that dragon, it's his choice, but he better do it on his time and money. If it wasn't for you he would be dead!" Fella said," I know I was stupid!" The more he talked the madder R got, R told DS to pull over, R pulled Fella out of the van. Fella tried to break off and run, R ran up behind him and shot him in his leg, Fella grabbed his left leg and fell over. R said," u dumb motherfucker I should kill u" and shot him again in the other leg. Fella was screaming," R I'm sorry man!" R then kicked him in his mouth breaking his front teeth. DS said," R come on let's get the fuck out of here, R got in the van, DS drove off. Looking out the window Carlos seen Fella trying to get up, R looks and starts to laugh. Not killing Fella was one of the worse mistakes R could have made.

Chapter 26

L was still pissed off about Shakim throwing water on him. He changed his clothes and was walking in the direction of the corner store to where his car was. He was about to cross the street when a black car pulled up, L got a funny vibe that street intuition started to rush in. L backed up some, Pop jumped out of the car with two other guys, L never seen before. Pop," L what's up kid?' L said," ain't nothing!" but stood his distance. L saw the imprint of a gun on Pop's waistband. L noticing that stepped beside a parked car.

Pop said," the word is y'all are doing good out here now." L said," you know the game." Pop said," nice chain you got on." L could feel the drama in the air it was so thick you could cut it with a knife. L said," what's this shit all about? I haven't seen you in mad years and you come around here like you're pushing up on somebody." Pop and the two dudes he was with pulled out, and Pop said, " L you know what this is!" L got behind the parked car the pistol was working its way out his waistband, Pop fired at him. Glass shattered above L from the parked car, L looked up Pop and his goons were running across the street at him. L cocked the gun, got up and started firing at them running side ways back into the block. The first few rounds made Pop duck down, the second blast that came from L hit Pop's man in the neck, the guy dropped the gun and fell down. L ran in the block, Pop and the other guy was still chasing him. The block was crowded, the sound of gunfire had mothers grabbing their strollers, everybody running in different directions, the veterans who seen this to many time just laid on the ground. They didn't want to start running and get hit with a bullet that wasn't meant for them. Although bullets don't have no name on them, L ran behind a tree and started firing back at them, Pop fired back and ran to the entrance of the first building, crouched low. Two police officers were checking a domestic violence call in the building a few doors down from where L was standing, they ran out the building both of them with their guns out one calling for back up and the other one yelling," drop the gun now and freeze." L turned to look, Pop opened fire on the two officers, and hit one of them in the chest. The cop he hit grabbed his chest, while going down he let off a few rounds. His partner opened fire on L, L tried to run but he couldn't, he felt himself falling, his legs numb, he put his arms up to block his face from the impact of the fall. L couldn't feel anything all he could hear was the sound of gunfire around him. Pop ran out the block with his goon right behind him, his goon turned around firing at the appearing cops, Pop jumped in the car and drove off. His comrade got hit seven to ten times before he went down. Before the gunfire stopped L passed out.

L woke up when he felt a hand on his shoulder, a paramedic was asking him was he in any pain. L," nah I don't feel shit right now. "The paramedic told him to be still and that he would be okay. L passed out again, they put a stretcher under him and put him in the ambulance. Once L got to the hospital they took him right to surgery.

L was awakened by the beeping of the heart machine. He struggled to lean up, his mother said "so you're final up, you been in and out of conscious since the surgery." L said," I'm in so much pain, call the nurse to give me something." His mother," she just gave you a shot of pain medicine, you can't get no more for a few hours." L said, "okay can you get me some water, my mouth is so dry." His mother left out the room and returned with a cup of ice water. Putting the cup at his lips she said," I told you this street life was going to get you killed or put you in prison. You're lucky to be alive!" "L, I'm sorry for all I put you threw." Putting the cup down, she placed her arms around his head and held him close, then said," hold on baby I just hope after all of this is over, you get your life together. They're charging you with murder and attempted murder on the cops. Those are very serious crimes." L looking down at the handcuffs on his right wrist thought to himself," damn I fucked up, it's over for me, ain't no changing my life." His mother said," they was trying to do the court arrangement from here, but you was in and out of it. Once they see you're awake and doing better it can be anytime now. The main doctor told me you were very lucky, one of the bullets just missed your spinal column. That's the reason you couldn't feel your legs at first, but you're going to able to walk." L," damn I'm lucky it was close." Mother," your father is coming to see you today after work, he been here since the beginning. I know it's been years since y'all talked, but he never stopped loving you it was your way of doing things we both couldn't stand. We both wanted the better things in life for you that was our main goal of working so hard, so we could leave them projects and give you something better." L was on the verge of tears, his mother seeing this said," get your rest baby, I know now is not the time for this, but it's going to be an long and hard road ahead for all of us and we'll be with you every step of the way." She kissed his forehead, saying goodnight and walked out the door closing it behind her.

DS, R, and Carlos were sitting at the table at R's crib. Carlos said," sun did u read that article about L in the daily news?" placing the newspaper on the table, DS picked it up," yeah I looked at it this morning. L is fucked up they didn't give him no bail or nothing! All we can do is pay for his lawyer." R," I went and got him Kaizer, I gave that motherfucker 40 grand and that's just for starters. Kaizer is worth every penny, he is a good lawyer. He beat my last case that shit with the cops, he got some personal shit against them.

" DS," now we gots to deal with Pop's ass, he got L into that shit and he's slowing down our paper and everything. He robbed Tank and some chick he was with, lucky Pop didn't shoot his ass." Carlos," we're going to bring it to his ass, we can't be sitting around waiting for this motherfucker." R," I'm already on top of that, Head's lil sister goes to that school on Main Street, once we get her we'll find Pop's ass."

There was a knock on the door, R pulled out the Mac and silently looked out the peephole. It was Tank, Born, Tommy and Lil Dee. R opened the door and let them in. Tank looking nervous said," yo what's up crew?" and everyone greeted one another with handshakes and high fives. R," what's up Tank? How did you let that nigga Pop get up on you like that?" Tank," Pop came out of nowhere, I was talking to Trina and that nigga came up behind me with three other dudes. I seen the look on that bitch face but I was to busy trying to get in her draws. Before I could do anything, they had took my gun, chain, watch and ring, along with $2,500. Pop told he the only reason I'm not dead is because he wanted me to give y'all a message. He said he wants y'all to pay him 20 a week or bodies are going to be all over the place. Then some dude he was with slapped Trina with the gun and took her earrings. I took her home, she was going crazy about calling the cops. I told her not to worry I'll pay for her earrings and shit. U know we don't want the cops in this anymore, I know the cops was asking L mad questions with the drama he's been going through, but you know he held it down."

R was furious R," don't you fucking go asking about my brother's integrity? I should slap the shit out of u!" DS went to calm R down. DS," walked R to the backroom," yo he just talking sun it's nothing." R," well if he ever use L's name in vain again I'll kill him." Tank was shook he never liked L, but he seen R's temper before. R stabbed a crack head for 5 dollars almost killing him, which Tank always thought, was nothing since he had mad paper. Tank knows R could flip over anything. Tank tried to apologize, but before he could say anything Tommy said," fuck Pop! We'll pay him alright with some hollow tips." That statement took R's mind off of Tank for now, R," lets grab that lil bitch cousin of his tomorrow." They all sat at the table and began laying out the plan.

L was sitting up on the hospital bed watching TV, the orderlies brought in a tray of food, put it on the table beside

L's bed. L lifted the top tray and looked down in disgust, this food was driving him crazy pudding and vegetables again. Just as he put the top tray back down his father walked in. He looked up in awe his father's hair grayed a lot and he put on a few pounds. His father walked up, gave him a hug, then shook his hands. His father was still heavy handed just like he remembered when he was younger.

His father," it's been a long time! I prayed for you since you made the decision to stay in Queensbridge. I knew in my heart something bad was going to happen to you out there, me and your mother did everything to make you change your mind, but you're mind was set. I'm sorry son I know you're going through a lot right now, how are you feeling?" L," I'm okay just sore like hell. They didn't give me any bail, so they are going to move me to the hospital at Rikers sometime next week. I know I did a lot of wrong and I'm going to accept all that comes my way like a man. You don't see all of the negative stuff when it's happening I'm sure nobody does, but that's the price you pay later on. I know you and mommy had the best plan laid out for me, but I took my own route and like a man I'm going to deal with it just like you told me." His father pulled up a seat next to the bed and they started to talk.

Chapter 27

Carlos went to his mother's apartment with DS, once he was inside Tracey and his mother was sitting down watching soap operas. Carlos went and sat between them, giving both of them a kiss.

He said," Tracey can I talk you in the back for a few, excuse me mom." His mother said," go ahead! Smiling at the both of them as they were walking back to his old room. Carlos sat on the bed with Tracey beside him. He said," Tracey, you, my sister, nephew and my mother have to leave here for now. It's to much going on and I don't want to see nothing happen to any of y'all." She said," what about school and everything I'm doing, I don't have anything to do with the shit you're doing in them streets." Carlos said," I know that the people I'm dealing with will do anything to hurt me or anyone close to me. I love you and don't want anything to happen to you. You could still go to school but not from around here" She said," okay Carlos just let me get my stuff together and I'll meet you back here." Carlos said," okay DS will take you there and back." Tracey kissed Carlos and went out the door with DS. Carlos locked the door and sat next to his mother," mommy I remember you saying that you wanted to leave from here, well I got you a four bedroom condo. It's all paid for and located in Long Island. So forget all your furniture and just pack your clothes." She said,' you're playing right! Carlos said," no" She jumped up and hugged him with so much joy. She said," I'm going to start packing now." Carlos just laughed and started to help her. He told his sister earlier that day, she was already there finishing up the last details of the new place.

A few hours went by and DS called the house phone to tell him to come downstairs. R and Tank helped him to the u-haul truck with his mothers belongs. Carlos, Tracey and his mother drove to the new place. His mother couldn't believe her eyes, the landscape surrounding the condo was beautiful. It was in a newly built complex, with a swimming pool in the back. It had a dishwasher, washing machine and dryer in the duplex. He made sure she had all top of the line appliances. It was a change from the projects. She was so happy and seeing this made him proud. His sister already had dinner on the table once they got there. Carlos brought all the bags in, then washed his hands so he could sit and eat. At the dinner table his mother said grace," God I think you for allowing my family to be together to enjoy this meal, Heavenly father thank you for the food today and watching over my beloved family, Amen."

After they all ate dinner Tracey and his sister put away the food and took care of the dishes. Carlos went upstairs to the bedroom, he turns the TV on to ESPN to watch the latest sports news. Tracey came up to the room. Carlos asked Tracey," do you like it?" She said," yes I do thank you." Carlos said," come walk with me downstairs I got something else for you." She said," okay" he held her hand and brought her outside the condo complex at the parking lot. Once outside he brought her to the far left side of the building and there was parked a red BMW with a ribbon on it. Tracey was overwhelmed, she kissed him and after the long embrace he handed her the set of keys. She took the ribbon off and placed it in the backset so they could go for a ride.

After they parked the new car in front of the condo they went upstairs to the bedroom. Damn! He thought to himself as she stepped out of the bathroom. Tracey had on a long see through white robe that curved to her hourglass figure. Her long black hair was still wet from her shower, imagine the anticipation he was feeling sitting across the room in the candlelight waiting on her to come out the bathroom. Baby girl walked to the radio to turn it on and the whispers CD was already to play, next she walked slowly to the bed kneeled down between Carlos's legs and unbuckled his pants, slowly she removed everything he had on and pushed him back on the bed. They began to kiss one another, he laid her on her back then gradually moved his tongue down until he reached her clit and licked her pussy until she exploded in orgasm and the cream slowly trickled out. She then grabbed his head for him to stop because the nerves were running though her body and she couldn't take it anymore. He then spread her legs open and slid his rock hard dick into her. He thrust his dick in and out to a motion that seemed to make her breathing quicken. Next he flipped her over so her beautiful ass could be up in the air and he could enter her from behind in the doggie position. He enjoyed teasing her slowly building her up to explode and then changing positions. They then went back into the missionary position. Their bodies glistened from the moonlight, they stroked each other, sliding up and down in the mixture of sweat and heated passion. They reached a climax at the same time, each stroke becoming harder and harder. The tingling sensation sent chills though their bodies as they continued the motion until they couldn't go any more. As she slept on his chest he knew in his heart that this was going to be their last night together. He gently moved her aside, got dressed went downstairs to get his suitcase, got his keys from off the dresser and got in his truck and drove back to the city.

Chapter 28

Tank pulled up in a blue van with police scanners blaring, there were a lot of 911 calls coming over the airwaves. R and Lil Dee got in R said," drive to Main Street. Every morning Head's sister Zora walks to school with her daughter Jasmine. We're going to grab both of them. Lil Dee you got the handcuffs and duct tape right?" Lil Dee," hell yeah nigga! Let's do this." Frank was walking down the block by the school dressed like a bum pushing an old shopping cart. As soon as he seen Zora and Jasmine coming his way his eyes lit up, he pushed the old cart their way. Once he got close enough to them he fixed his hat and blocked their path with the cart. The movement of his hat was the signal for Tank to pull up, Tank put the van in gear and slowly drove on the side on them. Zora said," hey what the fuck is wrong with u, you almost ran us over?" Frank said," sorry lady" acting drunk he quickly reached in his cart and pulled out a 12 gauge from beneath the dirty clothes and bottles. Zora was about to yell just as he grabbed Jasmine and put the gun to her head. Tank pulled along side of them, Lil Dee and R grabbed them in the van and sped off.

Carlos and DS was waiting impatiently for the phone call from R. Carlos wanted this to be over as fast as possible, he didn't like the idea of kidnapping the kid Jasmine who was only six years old, but in this game of high stakes anything goes. He knew this but it still bothered his conscious. DS was busy channel surfing when the phone rang, he let it ring five times before he answered. DS said," one" Carlos couldn't hear the conversation of the other end but he knew who it was. After hanging up DS said," let's go everything went right they got them in Brooklyn in the basement." Carlos," I gots to go to the bathroom first." DS," I'm going to get the car meet me in the front." And walked out. Carlos looked in the mirror at his own reflection, then went to meet DS.

Chapter 29

It had already been a long day for Carlos but the ride to Brooklyn was one of the longest journeys he had been on or at least that's how it seemed. DS parked his car a block away from the actual house, they walked there in silence. The smell of urine, dog shit and burnt flesh inflamed his nose and eyes, the mixture of those toxic smells almost made Carlos throw up. Carols held back the food he had eaten earlier, rats and cockroaches were all over the place." Like the smell? Asked R as he was standing near the bed were Zora and her daughter was tied at a bedpost. DS," did y'all find out where fucking Pop is at?" Carlos could see the fear in Tank's eyes, he knew R already did some unspeakable things, while looking at the burns on the little girls arms. R laughing like always said," yeah Zora told us where he's at, but first I want to make sure. D went to see if the information that bitch gave him was up to par!" as he was talking he went over to Zora and slapped her in the right side of her head with the pistol. Her head jerked up and down with the muffled sounds of a scream. Blood poured out of her right ear, she looked up at Carlos with fear and pain in her eyes.

Gloria and Tee pulled up at the address Zora gave them. Poppy's new Blazer jeep was parked in front of the brownstone. Pop was staying at this girl named Tonya's house, Gloria circled the block and parked a few houses down from Pop's jeep she was told to wait and make sure they had the right location. They waited patiently for Pop to emerge from the house door, as soon as he walked out a blue van pulled up. Pop walked to the van and they exchanged the basic ghetto greeting, Tee laid down in the backseat for fear of being seen. Pop knew him, but not Gloria. As the jeep and van drove off Gloria followed them and kept her distance. The jeep Pop was in turned right on Dekalb Avenue, Gloria and Dee headed back to where R, Carlos and Tank waited.

Gloria parked in front of the building, her and Dee got out. Dee knocked on the door. Tank answer and let them in. R" did y'all see that motherfucker." Gloria" yes, the address Zora gave is right on the money"

R smiled and said" that's the news I was waiting for" then walked back to the basement were Zora and her child was. R pulled a 10mm handgun and put it to Zora's face. Fear flushed her face, R gave her the reassuring look that everything was good'" you been a good lady, the shit you told me was the truth, like I told you if you did as asked I was going to let you and the lil girl go. R starts to untie her, R backs off and his pistols aimed at her, and he then tells her to untie her lil girl. R was close behind her. Zora was crying, as she takes the duct tape off her only daughter's mouth. R looks demonic at them, he says," get the fuck up both of you bitches!". Zora cuddled her lil one in her arms. Both of them in tears, you could see Zora was trying to be strong for her baby, she wiped the tears from her child eyes and told her everything was going to be all right. R said'" Zora you're going to put back on the blindfold if I'm going to let you go from here. Handing them to her. Zora had the look of revenge in her eyes from him, first she put them on her child's face, then her own. R'" pulled the chairs up and told them to sit. R" Carlos y'all get the fuck out of here I'll see y'all in the hood & stay the fuck on point" Carlos " okay sun see u later and call me when you get back out there." Carlos and everyone left but R and Gloria. Gloria went to lock the door, R was sitting in a chair in front of them. R grabbed the double-barreled shotgun and handed the handgun to Gloria. R put the shotgun to Jasmine's head then told Zora to take her blindfold off once she did R pulled the trigger, blowing Jasmine's face off the chair while the little girls body flew back. Blood flew all over Zora's body, she screamed out " no u motherfucker. Zora with hate in her heart ran to attack him and as soon as she did Gloria fired twice hitting Zora once in the neck and once in the chest, once she fell back Gloria fired two more times hitting Zora twice in the head.

Chapter 30

Carlos and DS pulled up in the projects, parked and headed to DS,s crib. Carlos fixed the handgun in his waistband and him and DS walked to his block. All eyes was on them as they walked threw the block. DS said, fuck these people out here and they walked in the building. DS unlocked the door, no one was there. DS put his gun down on the table then went to the back room to use the phone. DS called R.

DS" what's up kid did you handle your business?" R" yeah that shit is finished I offed both of them bitches and set the whole place on fire. DS' good no loose ends." R" you fucking know how I play." DS" yo what's the next move and most important how are we going to deal with Pop?" R'" you know I don't like the power of this shit being in his hands, I say we move on him as soon as possible, get the shit you need from there, then go see what's up with the workers and you and Carlos come to the safe house in Corona." DS' alright kid see u soon" then hung up the phone.

Carlos was lying down on the sofa watching TV, DS" lets bounce" DS put his hammer back on his waist and him and DS left. They left the crib and walked to see Ebony and Darren. Ebony was sitting on one of the benches on 10th street, Darren was standing there drinking a beer. Darren slapped both Carlos and DS's hand. Darren" what's up?" DS" how's things going?" Ebony said," shit today was the best day we had all week, all of that shooting had it hot like a motherfucker out here!!" Darren said" word! But it was a good day, the fiends were going crazy, they love this shit kid." DS started laughing" come on Ebony let's go count up and get the shit ready for Troy and them" (which was the next set of workers) Ebony and DS walked off, Carlos and Darren stayed on the block, Carlos sat down on the bench.

Carlos asked Darren" did u see Pop out here lately?" Darren said," nah, that motherfucker hasn't been around since the last shit he did" Carlos said, "you better stay on point for that dude" Darren said, "I know baby, I'm ready!" Carlos said," look out for Ebony too, make sure she gets home safe." Darren said, "without a doubt I walk her to her building every night." DS and Ebony got to her apartment in 40-09 10th street, Ebony put the key in the door and all they could hear was loud barking, it's her mean as hell rothweiler dog named Boss. As they enter Boss is jumping all on Ebony, Ebony pushes Boss off of her saying" be cool nigga jumping on my new shit, go in the room". Boss takes off running down the hall in the apartment into one of the bedrooms. Ebony follows him and locks the door, Boss just went in and shut it. DS is sitting at the dining room table, Ebony goes to the closet and opens the compartment of the safe, she gets out the money and brings it to DS. There's 10 stacks each and each stack has about 10 thousand dollars in each. DS" it's all here right?" Ebony " nigga don't play me like that, what the fuck is wrong with you." DS smiles then states" Ebony I'm just fucking with you, Ebony you know we're peoples" then pulls one of the rubber bands off one of the stacks and starts to count in. One thing about DS he didn't trust no one, but R, L and Carlos. DS and Ebony were walking out the building back to where Carlos and Darren were sitting. This blue unmarked detective car drives in the block at full speed, DS sees them and takes off running, they don't even bother to give chase, they stop by the bench were Carlos and Darren are sitting and jump out guns raised. Once they get out the car Carlos takes off, he runs towards the 12th street side entrance. A blue and orange patrol car is turning in, cuts him off. Carlos runs towards one of the buildings, he tries to turn the door but it was locked. The patrol cops got out with their guns out, Carlos put his hands up, the dees come over, Bundy and Thomas they are the assault squad. All the troublemakers or the known shooters they took down.

Bundy says" Carlos Cordero don't you fucking move, get on your knees with your hands raised." Carlos does as he is told. By now a little crowd is gathering. One of the cops push Carlos on the ground and put his knee in his back, the other one holstered his gun and starts to frisk him. He found a gun, and gave it to officer Bundy. He just smiles " got your ass" the uniform cop handcuffs him and they help pull him off the ground. Ebony starts going crazy yelling and screaming, "let him go you motherfuckers" trying to push Darren off of her. By now Miss Johnson and a few others are gathered around, the hood been like that since Richie got killed. Bundy called in for back up once he noticed how big the crowd was getting. All you could hear was the sirens of the arriving cops. As the uniform cop put Carlos in the squad car, Carlos yells at Ebony to be cool, he'll be all right. The sirens approached the crowed and used the sirens to part the group of people. Carlos looks out the back seat window, he noticed Pop and some dude with long dreads. Pop smiles a half smirk, half smile, then points his finger at Carlos with the gesture of a gun and pulls the trigger. Carlos just nods his head at Pop and the car pulls off. On his way to the 114t precinct Bundy reads him his Miranda rights. Carlos just sat there and listened his mind was on Pop.

Bundy parked the car in the rear of the building, he pulls Carlos out of the car and drags him to the desk sergeant. Sgt.," What pleasure do we have on bringing this guy in?" Bundy said," we caught him in possession of a firearm, Sgt. This is that asshole Carlos Cordero, him and his Lil posse are the ones doing all of the shooting down there in the fucking projects." Carlos said," I don't know what you're talking about" Bundy states," that's the word on the street fuck, now shut up." The Sgt had the look of happiness in his face. Sgt.," Bring his ass into the detaining area" Bundy hands his partner his firearm, then violently drags Carlos down the hall up some stairs into the detaining area. This room is dark steel grey, you can smell the mold, there is one door and a large table in the middle three chairs, one facing the mirrored wall the other two the other way.

Bundy's partner joins them there, Bundy un-cuffs Carlos and pushes him into the single chair. Carlos falls back his head hits the wall, he gets up and punches Bundy right in the nose, Bundy's head jerks back and blood pours out of his nose. Bundy 's partner hits Carlos in the head with a black jack, Carlos gets light headed from the blow, and he staggers and grabs a hold of the chair while trying to swing. By then the other uniformed officers heard the ruckus and rushed in. Carlos threw the chair in the direction of the oncoming cops, one of them squats it away, they all run in with nightsticks drawled and started hitting him, he tries to fight back but he blacks out. The Sgt. runs in " what the fuck are y'all doing? Let the fucking guy up. I been thru enough of this shit last year with the Richie Travel's case. Whoever the fuck this guy is a lot of people is out there and his lawyer is on the way. How am I going to explain this? Get him cleaned up right fucking now, while I get this fucking crowd to calm down. I'm going to have heads for this. Bundy was standing there holding his nose. The Sgt. Looked at him and said," go get cleaned up too!" Bundy walked pass him his face cherry red towards the bathroom. After Carlos got cleaned up they put him in one of the holding cells, Carlos didn't trust cops, they'll steal, sneak, and entrap. He'll never give them that ammunition to get into word play with him, he knew how they twist your words around every chance they got. He hated cops more than anything ever since they killed Richie. His lawyer came up to the holding cell to see him, lawyer" are you okay" seeing Carlos holding a towel against his head. Carlos says," yeah I'm cool, just get me to the court house so I can get the hell out." Lawyer" I'm going to stay here until they finish with the paperwork, prints and get you to central booking. I'll get you to see the judge before the day is over, did they put hands on you?" Carlos says," nothing I don't want to make a big thing out of this I just want to get out of here as fast as possible!" the whole time he was in the cops custody his mind was on Pop.

Chapter 31

Later that night after they arrived back in the projects, Darren walks Ebony back to her building. DS told them to make it an early night. Darren always walked her up to her apartment. Carlos had everybody on some walking up the stairs shit, except Ebony, she always took the elevator. As soon as Ebony got in the elevator Darren pulls out his hammer and walks up the stairs. Once Darren gets to the fourth floor, he noticed the hallway light flicking off and on. He sees two shadows in the corner and he sees a male standing by the elevator and a female on her knees. It wasn't uncommon for the fiends to turn tricks in the hallways or the elevator in the hood. Darren" who the fuck is that?" crack fiend Lisa sees the gun fear in her eyes, she yells," it's me Lisa." Darren knew Lisa his whole life, he knows she always doing shit like this. Darren said," hurry up and get the fuck out of this building" He wasn't trying to knock her hustle, he then turns to go up the next level of stairs, from the way Lisa and the trick was positioned Darren couldn't see the gun pointed at her neck. Darren laughed at Lisa, she was known for turning tricks anywhere. Once he turned to walk up the stairs the trick (Lloyd) runs up behind him and put the gun to Darren's head and takes the gun out of his hand. The trick says, "keep walking motherfucker make one mistake and you're dead". Lisa got up and ran down the stairs.

Ebony gets off the elevator, she doesn't always wait for Darren and begins to walk up the next flight of stairs towards her apartment. Ebony lives on the sixth floor, the elevators in Q.B. just go to the 5th floor. Pop and Greg was waiting for her on the next flight, the roof landing. As soon as Pop saw Ebony he and Greg ran down the stairs towards her. Ebony sees him but before she got a chance to move Greg hits her in the face with the weapon, Pop grabs her putting the gun to her head. Pop says," shut the fuck up and open the door bitch!" Blood pouring down her face, her hand was shaking, she was now wishing that she had unlocked Boss from out of the back room. She unlocks the door, Pop pushes her in, Lloyd is coming up the stairs with Darren, all of them went in the crib. Boss, Ebony's dog was barking loudly. Greg yells at Ebony and Darren to sit the fuck down. Pop pulls out two pairs of handcuffs and handcuff there hand behind them. Lloyd goes and turns up the radio, Greg puts duct tape on both of their mouths. Greg grabs a pillow from the couch and goes towards the barking dog, he opens the door Boss comes running out he fires two shots at Boss, Boss barks one time and goes down. Ebony knows what he's done but she doesn't want to believe it, she raised Boss since he was a puppy, she got him as soon as he was ready to leave his mother. She loved Boss, he was the only family she had except Carlos. She loved Carlos he always looked out for her after her brother Tee got killed in Maryland. After Tee got killed she moved back to New York, and Carlos looked out for her ever since. Pop slapped her in the face bringing her back to reality, Pop says" Ebony listen carefully what's the number to the safe. I'm only going to count on my finger zero to 9 and when I get to the right digit you nod your head" Greg pulled out a pen and paper. Pop says," u got what the fuck I said bitch, do u understand?" Ebony, tears running down her eyes nods her head in agreement. Pop says," good, I'm only going to do this once so no mistakes. If I go to open it up and its wrong I'm going to cut one of your boy here fingers off until we get it right do you understand. I don't got all day u hear me bitch. Are you ready?" Ebony nods her head then looks over at Darren, she sees the fear in his eyes. Ebony nods her head again, Pop pulls out his cell phone and dials a number. " Yo, blood you got the hoe Lisa with you? ok!" then he hangs up the phone and puts it back in his pocket. Pop says," ready!" Ebony nods her head once again. Pop does the hand gestures of numbers once he gets to eight Ebony nods and Greg writes it down. They continued this progress until Pop got the seven-digit number for the combination. Greg went to the safe and put the numbers in and the lock opened. His eyes lit up ever since he's been riding with Pop he's been starting to see money, he loved it. He took the money and drugs out of the safe and handed it to Pop. Pop says," good girl" then he kissed her on the cheek tasting her blood. Pop looked at Greg and Lloyd and said" y'all hurry the fuck up in here!!" Lloyd smiled ear-to-ear and dragged Darren into the living room telling Greg to turn Ebony around this way so she could watch. Greg duct taped both of Ebony's and Darren's legs to the chair. Lloyd put Darren in the middle of the living room. Pop said," I'm going to go to the van and wait for y'all" Pop knew what Lloyd was going to do, Lloyd was a bootie bandit when they was upstate in Sing Sing. Lloyd always raped some young kid coming in, he hated him but he knew he would have a good use for him on the outside that's why he kept him around.

Pop looked out the peephole then opened the door and went out with a bag of Ebony's drugs and money. Greg locked the door, then said" Lloyd we got us a party baby!" Lloyd pushed Darren on the floor ,Darren's face hit the floor hard. The duct tape muffled the sound of pain. Lloyd laughed and sat the chair up, Darren was lying face down on the floor. Fear and crazy thoughts were going through Darren's head, Greg put his elbow's on Ebony's shoulder, putting his weight down on her and held her head in the direction of Darren and Lloyd. Lloyd went into Ebony's bathroom, he came back with a jar of Vaseline and was holding a barber's razor in his hand. Ebony begins to try to move, Lloyd puts his stuff down on the table and kissed her on the cheek. Lloyd," watch the show baby after this you're next." Ebony moved her face away from him, she couldn't believe that this was happening to them, it was like she was in a distant dream, watching a sad movie that wasn't going to end until the sound of Darren's muffled screams, brought her back to the reality of what was happening.

Lloyd stood on Darren's back and pulled his cuffed hands straight upwards towards Darren's head. Darren's body jerked up and down until his arms snapped forward, Lloyd laughed at the sound of Darren's arm breaking, tears was running down Ebony's face she couldn't control it, she felt so sad for Darren. She loved him like a brother and she had terrible discomfort in seeing this happen to him. Darren felt this dude pulling his arms backward the pain was unbearable he cried out but the duct tape over his mouth stopped his out cry, he passed out from the pain, fear and shock. Lloyd pulled Darren's limp arms towards the radiator handcuffed them to it. Lloyd walked back to the table and grabbed the Vaseline and the knife and went back to the living room. Lloyd checked Darren's jean pockets, took out his wallet and look at the pictures in it. He took out the flick of him and his wife and son. Lloyd put the wallet in his back pocket, took Darren's pants down, grabbed the Vaseline and pulled out his dick. Greg put Ebony's face forwards the direction of Lloyd and Darren, she closed her eyes and Greg slapped her. He told her to keep her eyes open. Lloyd got off of Darren and pulled his pants back up. He went over to Ebony, a smile on his face" you're next honey." He went back to Darren and cut his neck from ear to ear, the first cut did it. Darren made some spastic movements, but not a sound came out of his mouth, once the movement stopped Lloyd un-cuffed him and dragged his limp and blood soaked body to the back room. Once he was walking back towards Ebony, she tried to move but couldn't. Greg laughed" your turn bitch…

My dick was hard the whole time thinking about what I'm going to do to u." Ebony let out her last tears, Greg pulled her towards the living room, she knew the fate that was about to take place. She put her faith in God to let her feel no pain and to let her make it through this. Lloyd pulled her chair into the living room cutting the duct tape that was on her legs freeing them. Greg" hold her down for me!" Lloyd smiled "of course!" Greg uncuffed her, she plunged out towards him, he said" oh you like it ruff" then hit her in the mouth with so much force she fell down. Lloyd was on her before she got to move again, he pinned her down, and he put his knees on her arms grabbing a hold on her neck. Lloyd said," bet you'll stop it now bitch, Greg lets go!" Greg pulled down her pants and underwear with not much of a struggle, he took off his pants and got on top of her. He ripped off her shirt and kissed her left breast, he put Vaseline on his penis for some moisturizer, he could feel her wet heat and he began to trust in her so hard he could feel her pelvic bone, he kept on with great urgency. His head went back and he let out a lil sound as he was cumming. When he was finished he got off of her. Ebony felt disgusted and was glad it was over, after Lloyd got off of her, she just laid there looking spaced out. Greg put his clothes on. Lloyd said," get up off the floor bitch!" Ebony struggled to get on her feet. Lloyd grab one of her marble statues and bashed her in the back of her head, she fell back down. He continued with blunt force until she didn't move any more. Lloyd and Greg got all of their belongings, Greg looked out the peephole and they both left to join Pop in the van.

Chapter 32

Bundy and his partner took Carlos to central booking in the Kew garden section of queens. Bundy said something on the radio and his partner got out to meet a uniformed officer and open the gate which we drove through, then it closed behind them. Bundy put the car in park and took Carlos out, into these double steel doors, then into a holding cell still handcuffed. There were seven other detainees in the cell. Carlos took a seat on the steel green bench that was attached to the wall. One by one they called the detainee's names out for the next progress, one of the hacks (court officers) called out Carlos Cordero! Carlos walked to the cell door the hack walked him into a part where a male officer stood behind a huge desk. There was an x on the floor and the officer directed Carlos to stand on it. The officer" looked at the x on the wall and told Carlos to stand still" then snapped a photo of him. The officer then directed him to turn to his left. After both photos were taken they lead Carlos to another desk where the officer who took him out of the cell un-cuffed him. The hack behind the desk told him to take everything out of his pockets, off with his sneakers and to put them on the desk where they could be seen and then they strip-searched him. After that part was done they took him into another part which was where Carlos was seen by a doctor, the doctor asked him question about his health and if he was feeling alright. The next stop was the bullpen, There was close to 45 detainees in there even though the maximum capacity was set for 20.

One by one their names were called to be screened by a social worker, who asks their address, date of birth, jobs, next of kin and shit like that. This allows the District Attorney to screen you for bail or to see if the person has community ties, most of the time they want to see if anyone loves you in the free world. All of this was just bullshit once they pulled your jacket. They know what they are going to do to you from the jump, but there's nothing you can do but go along with their bullshit program. Carlos been in their institutions a few times and the same rules always applied.

Always walk light and be ready to move fast. If you're active in the streets, you're going to jail. If you don't you're either lucky or cooperating (snitch) with the police. A lot of dudes get caught with all types of shit and most people don't understand why they come right out and luck doesn't have nothing to do with it. When they moved Carlos to the next cell there was this monster of a dude sitting on the bench by himself, although it was very crowded in there. Carlos walked over to the bench, the dude looked up, studied his face for a second, and... connected. Flashing to where they started. They were in this youth institution a few years back,

Orange town. Carlos was in there doing a year for a robbery, big Tony was there for cutting his mother's boyfriend. Tony was always a big guy even back then. He was 15 years old, the biggest guy in the place, he had heavy cheekbones, dark eyes, a thick Afro, a calm interior stillness radiating off him. His skin a faint coppery tone, you could tell he was mixed. Carlos later found out his mother was Spanish and his father black. They had met in the yard working out. Carlos had met him through a dude from the hood, and they just took a liking to one another. He was later placed on the same work detail as me, and in there you had to work and go to school. They both worked in the mess hall for 10 cent a hour, it wasn't much but it made the day go by.

One day back at the dorm, it was none of his business, when Macho and his gang tried to jump on this dude Eugene, but when Eugene broke free and ran, he headed straight to Carlos's bunk. Macho and his boys were right behind him, taking their time, laughing, knowing nobody was going to come in and stop them. A few screams in that place wouldn't raise an eyebrow, much less a guard. Carlos didn't know why but he just snapped because one of Macho's partners was on Eugene. Carlos grabbed the homemade knife from his boot and stabbed Macho's partner in the arm, and he turned and ran. Macho was pounding Eugene's face into a pulpy mess, giggling. Carlos nailed Macho in his shoulder with the knife, but he was way tougher than his partner, because he grabbed Carlos's arm and flipped him over. Macho was on top of him trying for his throat, he kept trying for Macho's eyes, but he'd been there before and easily block him, all of a sudden big Tony came and grabbed Macho from behind in a choke hold pulling Macho and Carlos up at the same time. Carlos never seen such strength. They heard the whistle and knew the guards were coming. Nobody would tell what happened and all of them ended up in solitary, they knew no one would talk, they all came up in the same type of places.

They shipped all of them to different joints. Tony got off the bench and gave Carlos a handshake and hug, it's been years since they last seen each other. Carlos said" Tony, what's up brother been a while!" Tony replied" truth to that, so we're back on the inside!" Tony sitting back down, Carlos right by his side, Tony asked" what you in for this time?" Carlos answered " I got a firearm beef, no big thing I got one of the best lawyers in queens so I should be cool, what about you?" Tony said," a minor fist -fight but with my record who knows how it's going to turn out. I was bouncing at this bar on Parsons Blvd. and I tried to kick this asshole out and he took a swing at me, so you can imagine the rest." Carlos just laughed, Tony said" I hit him with a one hitter quitter, he folded like a folding chair, and his friend hailed down a passing police car. But since it was a white feller here I am." They continued to talk about everything until they dozed off. Carlos was awakened by the sound of the morning breakfast cart coming around, they always gave you the same thing cold cereal, low fat milk and a fruit. After breakfast was done the public pretenders (defenders) come around looking at detainee's cases. Carlos's lawyer Kaizer came and called him into a small booth. Kaizer said," you okay I'm going to get you out of here fast. DS, your girl and mother are out there. DS said don't worry about it whatever the bail is you're out today." Carlos said," let's get this shit on, also pull my man Tony Yardley's case I got the fee for it he's an old friend can't let these legal Bengal's handle it." Kaizer said," let's just get you out of here first" Carlos said," of course, do your magic" Kaizer just laughed, grabbed his folder and left the booth. Carlos went back into the cell arena to see Tony. Carlos said" Tee I got my lawyer to try to pull you out of here, so just sit back let the cards play." Tony said, "Los I don't know what to say!" Carlos stopped him before he could continue and said," it just a debt paid back." They both sat back down, a half of hour went by and one of the hacks called out" Carlos Cordero" Carlos got up to walk to the cell door, he gave Tony a pound and said" see you on the other side this time!" Tony said" good luck brother!" Carlos walked out to this little hallway to a big brown door to the courtroom. The hack walked him in front of the judge's bench. Kaizer and the D.A. on both sides of me. The court officer said" face the judge with both of your hands behind you." Carlos gave him the look of been there before and he backed off. The judge said," violation of the penal law 102.3, criminal possession of a firearm in the 1st degree. What is your case D.A.?" D.A said." well the people are asking for the bail of $ 25,000 because of his prior convictions, he was caught with the weapon on his persons." The judge said," Counsel" Kaizer said," as you could see my client has good community ties, his mother, wife and friends are here in this courtroom now " gesturing for them to stand and continued" his prior sheet has nothing to do with this case your honor, as you are aware of all the police misconduct in the area he was arrested in!" the D.A. said," that has no grounds for what this man was caught with, officer Bundy has an unparalleled record your honor" the judge said " okay this is just an arraignment not a trial, let's just set the bail at $15,000!" Kaizer said," thank you your honor his family is here to pay the bail now." The judge said," we'll set the next date for two weeks from now. Kaizer turned to Carlos" just go in the back until all of the paperwork is done." The judge said next case, the court officer brought Carlos back into the holding area. Carlos walked back into another cell but once the guard left he called out to Tony." Everything is good my peoples are posting my bail now" Tony screamed back out to him" that's good bro" Carlos" don't worry Kaizer got you!" Tony was arraigned and bail was $500 dollars. Carlos tells the lawyer to pay the bail for him and tell him once he was released to come to the projects to meet up with him.

Chapter 33

Tank and Flo was standing on the block it was pouring down raining, crack fiends were lined up!

Tank says," cop and go!" as one fiend Michele is pleading for another piece. Tank yelling tells Michele to keep it moving. Michele pleads," come on Tank as much money as I spent tonight, it's raining there isn't any dates coming." Michele was one ugly motherfucker but she always finds dates to pick her up. Mostly white businessmen. Tank tells Flo to give her a extra one. Tank says" u better bring me back that money later or I am going 2 fuck you up!" Michele gets the other piece of crack rock and says," you know I am good for it, thanks baby see y'all later." and runs off. Rain, sleet nor hail will stop these motherfuckers from using! There was this fiend named Jackie that use to bring her three year old daughter with her to cop, literally carrying her to the dealers on the block. Tank was bugging when he seen that the little girl told him," give my mommy a big one" Tank kicked her off the block and told her to never come around with that baby anymore. R started the whole projects selling crack loose, they did without the vitals and plastic bags. It made it easier to get the product on the streets faster, also it saved all of his workers from getting arrested, in not having vitals or bags. They would carry it in tic tac boxes the spearmint ones, the dumb ass cops thought they just had tic tac's and let them go, until a rat put them up on that.

Tank says," damn sun it's fucked up, what happened to Darren and Ebony, shit I am scared to be out here with that dude Pop still running around" Flo said," that dude is serious!" Tank says," I feel the same way, any dude that comes around that I don't know I am shooting first and asking question later" Tank gave Flo a pound and says" me too sun!" As they was talking Lucky walked up.

Lucky was a childhood friend of theirs he just got out of the system (jail) for a robbery gone bad. Tank says," what's up kid?" and gives Lucky a pound. Lucky replied, " what's going down sun?" Flo said," just hanging on the block getting this dough," Lucky said" I heard y'all were doing big things when I was up north. I heard thru the wire about R, DS and Carlos rocking the whole hood." Tank said," that's the truth there sun, we got this shit locked down" Flo was starting to feel a vibe from Lucky although they grew up together, he knew Lucky never like DS nor Carlos and now for him to come around with all these praises for them wasn't feeling right. Flo said," Lucky that's how this shit is going sun, anyway what's up with you?" Lucky said," man I just got out a few days ago, I been trying to get up with Los and them to see where I fit in" Tank said," well sun and them don't be around here like that, but if you give me a number or something I will get it to them?" Lucky said" yeah I got one, my shortie got me a cell phone so give them this number 7182327689", tell DS, R or Los to hit me. How's L's case looking?" Tank said, " he blew trial and got 20 years!!, But he got a few beatable things in his case so he should give that back." Lucky said," word that's fucked up, I was with a few dudes that was with him on the island and sun was holding it down, even through we had that fight we was still peeps." Flo didn't change his facial expression he remembered it was no fight as Lucky said it was just an old fashion ass whipping, and Lucky got it. It was like stepping between the ropes with a prizefighter for Lucky. Shit it seems like L had four arms, as fast as he was throwing them combos, all Lucky could do was cover up and try to protect his self, but as soon as there was an opening L's fist hit the target. All that mess Lucky was talking before they squared up was gone, once Lucky dropped his guard L was all over him, all Lucky could do was go along for the ride. Should of seen his face the joy in his eyes, when Carlos got L off his ass. Tank said," I will make sure sun gets your number to holla at you." Lucky gave them fives and walked back out the block.

Flo said," yo sun I am not feeling Lucky he got a trick up his sleeve cause something about him wasn't right." Tank said in Lucky's defense" nah sun you are bugging, Lucky is a good dude." Flo said," I am telling you sun, you know you got to go with your feelings out here" Tank said" I feel you I am going to call R up now" he pulled his cell phone out his pocket and called R, he knew better than to give Lucky anyone's number without calling first. He was a lil scared of Pop from the stories he heard, but he witnessed R's actions first hand. R picked up on the second ring, R said" yo!!" Tank said," it's me Tank, everything is going as planned on the block but Lucky came around looking for you, DS, and Los" R said, " word what the fuck that dude want?" Tank," he was trying to get up with y'all, that's all he was basically saying, I guess he is looking for some work or something" R said," oh yeah, I am not feeling that cat since that shit with L, he really must want to get murdered or something" R said laughing. Tank said," I don't know sun just passing the message" R hangs up. Flo is wondering what R said so he asked" what R said?" Tank said," he isn't fucking with dude!!!"

Lucky walks in the corner store and asked the store clerk for change of a dollar, the clerk gives him change. Lucky walks to the corner phone and dials Pop's number. The phone rings Pop answers, " I kill them you chill them" Lucky laughs and says, " what's up thun?" Pop says," who is this another dead man on the line," Lucky says," it's Lucky!" Pop says," what's up comrade?" Lucky says," I did as you asked comrade them dudes are acting like they didn't see them around lately, but you know I am going to play the part with you until we get all of them niggas, as far as I am concerned even L in lock up too!" Pop starts laughing," you know it off with all of their heads!"

Chapter 34

Los just got out the shower, walked to the bedroom thinking the bullpen shit sucks being stuck in there for a few days without a shower. He remembers this guy from the hood that did 15 years in various state jails and the first thing he wanted before a woman was a hot slice of pizza and to dodge traffic on 21st street (which is a 4 lane street about 100 square feet), that thought always stuck in his head. Los's whole life has been a repeat of this. Anybody he knows at least been arrested once, sometimes for nothing, sometimes for the worse shit on this planet and a lot of times for bullshit! Tracey comes in the room and says," are you okay Ms. Pat and them was going crazy, make sure you call her and tell her you are ok.!" He said," just some bullshit, they got me with a biscuit (gun), the worse case scenario was a year in jail but with Kaiser he works magic in that court room, you know!" Tracey said, " babe why you don't walk away, we got a lot of money saved and I'm going to have a good job after this semester, we can just stay away from there, no one knows us here" she starts crying. Los said, I don't know maybe it would work. Tracey felt it or knew if he walked out that door, he wasn't come back to her. Sometimes a woman's (intuition) was like that. Los was so caught up in getting Pop that there was no turning back. Since he killed Ebony, Carlos had been having dreams and thoughts of killing Pop, nothing nor no one was going to change him and Pops destiny.

Los's phone rang, Tracey was looking at him while silently praying he didn't answer it. He reached for the phone and as he answered it he walked toward the bed. The look in Tracey's eyes hurt his soul knowing it was something that was going to take him out of her life. Carlos answered knowing it was R, He said," what it is?" R said," shit, sun time to click that clock!" Carlos said," where am I meeting you at?" R said," the spot in Corona!!!" Carlos hung up the phone to finish getting dressed, after he got dressed he walked up to Tracey, she gave him a hug and kiss, he reached in his pocket and gave her a gold key in a locket with a piece of paper. Looking in her eyes telling her to hold on to this Carlos said," I will see you later, Tracey kissed him then said" I love you so much babe" he walked downstairs, the smile on his mother's face playing with his nephew was so beautiful, he didn't want to disrupt the peace on it so he just walked out the door.

Chapter 35

R was in the house in corona, pacing around with a 9mm glock 21 shotgun in his hand, talking on the phone.
His girl Gloria was on the sofa watching the daily soap operas she loved. Gloria said," stop walking around you are going to burn a hole in the floor." R said," shut the fuck up!!! I am waiting for Paco to bring the work, I been waiting for his call." Gloria said," he is going to call just chill the fuck out!" Gloria walked in the kitchen and brought R back a Budweiser, opening the cap she handed it to him. R drank some then sat down while waiting for the phone to ring.

Carlos pulled up to the spot on 112th and 41 Avenue, Carlos sees R's hot rod black maxim. R had fixed it up with hydraulics, a powerful v8 FSI engine that allowed the car to accelerate from 0 to 62 mph in 4.6 seconds with the top speed of 185 mph. It was equipped with bulletproof windows and doors, and had a gun stashed behind the glove compartment. R has been driving that car lately so he can be ready if he runs into Pop. One thing Carlos learned about R is he liked killing. Carlos walked up to DS to give him a pound" what's up thun?" Carlos said," aint shit my dude" DS said," Wanda sends' her regards. How's moms doing?" Carlos laughs," Moms is fine!! How's the warden Wanda doing? I am surprised she let you out the house!" DS pushes him in the chest and they grab each other laughing, and then give one another a brotherly hug and walk in the house. R is sitting on the couch

R said," what's up comrades?" yelling out to Gloria - bring some more beers," Carlos and DS are here!" Gloria goes into the kitchen and brings the beer to them as she greets them, then she goes back to the backroom. R said,' this fuck Paco didn't call yet!!!" before he can finish the phone rings" R answers " aceptar este/a epoca perrorra!" Paco tried to talk but R cut him off R said," acasco" Paco tried again R continues," escuchar" Paco was quiet. R said," bien amigo you got my dinero fucker! My papel, is that a damn problema? Are we claro, all I needed was for you to llamar, do I have preguntar for that. A lil communicacion to know you're seguro! Why amigo every time I deal with u, I got to show fuerta, I am waiting for you to llegar, I am ready to matar and for Guerra! Paco' said." ok ok!!"

R hung up the phone and started smirking then picks up his handgun. He places it in his waistband and walks to the front door. R tells DS," I will b right back bro!" R walks to the front to a gray van, Paco gets out. R says," like I told you bro, you fucking call me and let me know something, I don't like to b waiting!!!!" R could see the fear in Pacos eyes, he was getting a kick out of it. Paco says," sorry it will never happened again, it's just my phone battery went dead!" Paco knew of the treachery and ruthlessness that R displayed on some of the jobs he accompanied R on for the boss Miguel Cadena. Cadena was the head of the Cadena cartel.

Paco wanted to ease the tension, so he walked back to the van and got the duffle bag out the back and handed it to R. R says," fucking wait here Paco I'll b right back" with a smirk on his face. R went in the house and locked the door behind him. Paco went and lit a Marlboro cigarette. R went to the kitchen to put the duffle bag on the island. Carlos and DS followed him in there. R unzipped the bag and started taking the kilos out counting them, he handed them to Carlos, and Carlos placed it by the stove and got the scale out of the cabinet above the sink. Carlos grabbed a knife and carefully opened it. Carlos placed a plastic sandwich bag on the scale, he weighted out 50 grams, then put another baggie on the scale and weighted out 20 grams of baking soda. Carlos went under the sink and got the coffee glass pot and put both the baking soda and the coke in there. He turned on the front stove eye, turned on the hot water put a lil in the coffee pot, stirring the mixture together. Carlos started to slowly swirl the pot around the heat and hot water. This made the mixture of cocaine and baking soda turn into a lightly colored gel close to eggshell white. Some of the particles loomed on the top of the water. Carlos took the pot off the fire, spinning and blowing into the water to make the particles drop down into the gel. The gel gets shaped circular like the indent of the bottom of the pot. Carlos puts the pot down and waits for it to dry. Once the gel turns hard and dries it is shaped like a big cookie. Carlos pours cold water into the pot and takes the crack cookie out and places it on some bounty paper towels. When it dries he then puts it on the scale, it weights 49.0 from 50 grams. Carlos said," R this is it, what we need bro!" R said," good so it was worth the wait huh!" Carlos said," without a doubt!" R puts the remaining fourteen kilos back into the duffle and walks out to Paco, whom he had waiting for the last 35 minutes. R says," Paco my man" his whole demeanor changed since their first meeting. Paco gets out the van, R hands him a black book bag. R said," tell Miguel he will have his other half in a few days like always" Paco said," of course!" takes the bag, gets in the van and drives off.

R stands there watching until the van is out of his sight, then walks back into the house. R says," I am going to get Tank and the crew so they can get started on this shit, y'all could stay or go if you like, you know I don't stay for this shit but I am today." DS says laughing I am outta here comrades, going to take the wife and kids to the movies and dinner!" Carlos says, " yeah we know who the boss is" DS laughing says," I told you about that shit" Smiling Gloria walks in on the conservation Gloria says," DS you better not say anything about my girl it only takes a second to dial, I will be right on the phone with her!!" DS says," now why would I set myself up and do that!" everyone bust into laughter. DS gave Gloria a departing hug, Gloria said," tell my girl to call me, if she don't I will b by the house." DS said," I sure will Gee" R said," alright now sweets get in there and start separating the work up" Gloria left them in the living room and walked to the kitchen. DS, R and Carlos all slapped each other fives and DS walked out the door, Carlos locked it. Carlos went in the kitchen and started helping Gloria.

Chapter 36

Detective Bundy and Det. Franco were in a dark tan sedan stuck in heavy traffic on the BQE expressway. Bundy said," use the fucking sirens already! Put the Fucking God damn sirens on, you know I hate fucking traffic! Plus we been trying for the last six months to see agent Crowley about this case." The person in the back seat says," yeah I want my fucking dough and a way out of this case I got, plus to be relocated." Franco says," okay-.okay!" Franco then put on the siren. The siren's squeal split the morning, the flashing blue-then-red-then-blue dashboard lights reflected off the other cars as they weaved their way through rush hour traffic. They rode pass three more exits until they arrived at Tillery street. They exited the expressway and drove pass four lights until they hit Jackson street.

The dark sedan pulled up to Janet Crowley's assigned parking spot. Janet Crowley was a stunning beauty of 5 feet 5 inches, with dark complected skin and long black wavy hair. She was a single black FBI agent with no boyfriend. Her last two dates was of both races white and black. She was unsatisfied by both. Most of her college and high school life was the same. She was a high-strung lady, she was very studious, reading every book she got her hands on. She won all of her debates in high school and college, and graduated the top of her class. She was a no nonsense woman, which drove a lot of people away from her, men and woman alike. In her mind she was always right and she took honor in arguing nonstop to get her point across. Then the next day she would bring her textbook or print out information, which assured what she was saying, was correct. She would get her facts from the world wide web to prove her point, she was seldom wrong. She was a human almanac, she knew facts about every topic or subject.

Janet Crowley didn't drive, so she told Bundy to park in her spot. She just kept the spot for the power of it, she was a very power driven woman. Bundy approached the dark haired secretary's desk. Bundy said," hello I am Det. Bundy to see agent Crowley." She replied, " hold on sir" she picked up the phone and hit a button. "Det. Bundy here to see you" Crowley said," send him up" Crowley stood up and brushed the lint and other particles she could see off her black suit and sat back down. Bundy got off the elevator on the fifth floor and went to the receptionist desk," I'm here for agent Crowley" the receptionist said, "the door to the left, right to the back. Crowley 's office was located in the corner of the building, her view was lovely and the décor tastefully placed. Bundy knocked on the door, Crowley said, "come in" Bundy opened the door and walked in. Bundy said," hello agent Crowley" Crowley replied," nice to see you detective Bundy."

She got up to greet him they exchanged firm handshakes. She didn't like Det. Bundy since her last case in the 114th precinct district. She thought he was an asshole then and more of an asshole now. Her dislike for him was displaced in her tone and her demeanor didn't show it. Crowley said," so it's been brought to my attention the case you was bringing up, so you went over my head, now that's how we do things now, I thought we had a better relationship then that." Smirking Bundy said," no Madame I would never do that and handed her the files" she loves to see him squirm. Bundy said," these are the files on the guys I was telling you about, but the great thing now is we got a eyewitness.

Look at this file he pointed to the one that had Frank Fermin aka Fella on it, he wants to make a deal. Bundy said," not only can he tell us about the inside work, but he was also a shooting and robbery victim from this one Ricardo Rodriguez aka "R" . Crowley said," let me look at these files" Crowley was overlooking the files she couldn't believe some of the things she was reading. "You mean to tell me this group of guys are responsible for turning the number up (crime rate) in your district. You got murder, robbery, drugs and countless other things on these guys and your guys didn't bring them in?" She was furious, Bundy said," we only got one of them on a weapons charge. Carlos Cordero. We couldn't get them on nothing but a few minor arrests.

Nobody was giving us the info we needed to get them all. Down in them projects the stigma of being seen as a snitch or the fear of retaliation prevents many from testifying about even the worst crimes. Most of the leads we had fizzled! That's why I been trying to bring the case to you, I got to admit that I screwed the car shop case up, when you told me to back off, I should of, I just wanted to arrest these guys and I want you to know that I'm going to make sure they never get out of prison." Crowley said," let the past be as it is, but only keep in mind I told you so" with a strange look on her face" lets get started on this"

Bundy said," well we have Frank Fermin downstairs we picked him up from Rikers island earlier" Crowley commanded" bring him up and I am going to get the DA on the phone, I am going to do everything by the book to make sure this case sticks." Bundy said," ok" Crowley pressed the intercom, "Maria set up an interview room in 10 minutes please!" Maria said, " yes boss" Bundy called Franco on his two-way radio. Franco said," yeah" Bundy said," bring him up!" Franco looked back at Fella. Franco said" u ready" Fella," yes" he nervously replied," can I have another smoke before we go up?" Franco got out of the car and took Fella out. Franco said," listen I am going to cuff you in the front so just relax" Fella," yes sir" after he had him cuffed in the front Franco reached into his pocket, took out a box of Newport and gave Fella one. Franco sparked the lighter and lit Fellas Newport, Fella inhaled deeply. Fella said," I want my deal in writing from the DA and judge, and I want this drug case to disappear!!" Franco says," we'll let's get it done." After Fella stomped on the Newport, Franco led Fella into MDC the Federal Bureau of Investigation.

Chapter 37

Carlos called DS " yo what's up thun?" DS said," are u going to hit the club with us tonight?" Carlos said," for sure thun we are going to buy the spot out, every bottle of champagne they got" DS laughing," of course that's without a doubt my dude, that's how we do it". Carlos asked," what time are we riding out?" DS said," like 10 so we can get in the spot early and wild out." DS always went to the Vixen bar early, his dude Barkim was the head dude at the door so they always got to bring biscuits in the spot. DS said," I spoke to Jewel, Cash, Don, Teik and they're going to meet us up there. Teik was a trigger- happy dude, him and Jewel just liked to kill and rob. Most of the time for the smallest things. Teik has always been a dangerous dude all his life. All the hoods that were within a 20-block radius knew that. That's why him and Jewel were the best of friends you never knew when one of them was going to do something.

Teik was a brown skinned, slim built guy with a deadly hand game, he knocked a lot of dudes out for sleeping on his small frame. One day Teik was walking his daughter to the store and this cat Gary was with his dog. A jet-black, diesel pit bull, Gary always had his dog off the leash and Teik talked to him once before about that. He told that dude to keep his dog on a leash it is a lot of lil kids and older people out here and the dog is scaring them. Gary was a dude with a smart-ass mouth but he was pussy, always hitting girls and shit. Gary got nine sisters so of course there's female ways in him.

Gary" I told you my dog ain't going to do nothing unless I tell him too, so I don't have to put him on no leash". Teik was with his daughter, so now wasn't the time "ok I feel u, no big deal kid." The tension was full, Teik walked off scheming. The next night there was a light drizzle coming down, Teik was parking his Nissan Z and he saw Gary chaining his pit bull to the fire hydrant by the store. Teik sits waiting for Gary to go in the store, Teik gets out of the car and walks to Gary's pit and shoots him twice in the head. Gary and everybody in the store heard the gunshots and ran out the store. Gary sees his pit bull in a pool of blood and cartilage all over the place. Gary starts running and crying for his dog. Teik is standing there laughing, Gary looks up and sees Teik. Teik said," didn't I tell you about that fucking dog!" And walks in the project.

They all meet up at the club at 9:45. DS walked over to Barkim and escorted them into the club pass the heavy line that was forming, without searching them. Don was the first one at the bar, he grabbed the fine bartenders arm, "hey sweets, can I get 10 bottles of Don P?" she said" you know they are 500 a bottle?" Don says," well if that's the case make it 12.!!!" And pulled out a wad of hundred dollar bills. R was just laughing at Don, R said to Don" lets get right!" It was a lot of beautiful woman in attendance that night, it was 6 females to 1 guy. Carlos knew tonight was going to be a good one. Don had his crew from Far Rockaway with him, R had his shooters from Bushwick, Jewel had his crew from the Bronx with him and Teik had some Fort Greene dudes with him. They were like 70 strong in that spot. The night was going great R was dancing with a fat ass Spanish chick, things was good. A few hours later Carlos sees Tank and he got Lucky with him. Tank and Lucky walked over to the VIP section they're are in. Tank" gives Los a pound so does Lucky. Lucky says," what's up Los" Carlos says," Eaze what's the deal with you?" Carlos didn't like Lucky since the fight between him and L, he knew Lucky held a grudge. R wanted to rock him but Carlos didn't think it was worth it. Carlos didn't over-estimate or under-estimate Lucky, he just didn't trust him. Carlos said," we was just about to blow this joint" R always wanted to leave the club early before it closed because that's when most of the madness happens, when the party's over. Lucky says," damn we just got here" Carlos took the last remaining bottles from the table and handed them to Lucky. Lucky asked," when are we going to get up, I got some things to holla at you bout?" Carlos said," we will get up soon" just as him and everyone they were with was leaving the club. Lucky stayed behind smirking, thinking he can't wait to see his acquaintance Pop.

Chapter 38

It was scorching hot outside, DS and his son was playing catch football in the backyard. DS didn't notice this white carpet cleaning van parked across from his yard. Ty was driving that commercial van, Ty drove slowly down the block again. Pop was looking at DS playing with his kid. Pop had the look of amazement, Pop laughing" don't that lil fuck, look just like him? It's so fucking funny, let me tell you that chick Camilla gave Lucky the info on the nose." Camilla once was one of Wanda's best friends, but they grew apart. Camilla felt it was DS's fault, she felt like DS took her only friend in the whole world. Camilla gained weight, she was heavily depressed, and thinking everyone she interchanged with was against her, her whole family had a history of mental unstableness. When Lucky started to show her a lil love, she was overjoyed. Little did she know, Lucky was being deceitful all he wanted was all the information he could get from her so he could pass it on to Pop.

Chapter 39

This is precisely the info Pop needed, where one of his most distinguished enemies lived. Before Pop heard about his uncle, Pop actually liked DS, even through DS was younger than him. He admired the way homey moved. But now all he was fascinated about was the conflict he was having with R, Los and DS. He embraced it, it kept him going. Pop loved his uncle more than anyone in his family, the many juvenile facilities and state jails he was in, his uncle raised him along the way. Today was the day that he was going to get one of the ones responsible for taking his uncle away from him, he couldn't wait, but Pop learned to be a patient man. He once read this quote in one of the many books he consumed up north (beware the anger of a patient man) also (anger and haste hinder good judgment).

Pop was a very patient man, once he had a beef with this dude Clark from the projects and he strategized his next move. Pop waited in the slop sink, the cleaning supply room, which are on the first floor in all of the Queensbridge housing buildings. Clark's apt was on the first floor right across from the cleaning supply room, Pop sat in there looking out a slim crack of the door for almost 50 hours (the porters didn't work on the weekends). When Clark final came out Pop jumped out and stabbed him in his back 10 times, then ran up the stairs and crossed the roof to his aunt's crib. Clark succumbed to his wounds, the fatal mistake Clark made was to disrespect Pop's girl Ciara. Ciara was the love of Pop's life, even thru all the time he was away, she never left him, she was on the visit every other weekend or every weekend depending which jail he was in. Pop had undying love for her and for him to let any walking person male or female disrespect her wasn't going to happen and for that Clark lost his life.

Pop was determined to get DS, Carlos and R they had to pay. DS threw the football to his son Darius, Darius was the splitting image of him, he had cornrows in his hair just like DS. DS said," come on lil Dee, daddy gots to go, let's get ready so I can bring you to grandma's!" Darius playfully tried to run pass him, DS said," no you don't" picked Darius up and put him over his shoulder, then patted his behind while carrying him into the house. Forty minutes later DS and Darius walked to DS's black BMW. DS put Darius in the backseat, placed the seatbelt on him and put the overnight bag in the trunk. Wanda was standing by the front door, she was five months pregnant with their second child. DS went to kiss and hug his wife goodbye then rubbed her belly, she was carrying big like she was nine months. They just went to get a sonogram, they was expecting a girl, that's exactly what Wanda wanted. DS wanted another boy but he was happy with whatever it was going to be. DS said," love you babe, see you later." Wanda says," "love you daddy, be safe." DS says,"" I will sweets." DS jogged back to the car and started it. DS black on black chromed out BMW traveled on to the Brentwood exit of the L.I.E (long island expressway). The white van followed, Pop said," keep up with him, I am going to blaze duke on the grand central right before the interboro." Traffic was very light in the mid afternoon. DS turned onto the grand central parkway Pop reached into the glove compartment and took out two chrome 45's, Pop put one in both of the heads. Pop says," pull along the side of thun" Ty pulled on the side of DS's car, Pop put both guns on the door and window panel and opened fire. DS didn't hear the first gunshot cause the music was up, the second shot shattered the drivers side window, DS tried to duck down but to no avail, Pop kept firing. The first fatal shot hit DS in the neck, and then the side of his face and the rest riddled his body. The BMW lurched forward hitting another on coming car, jumped the curb and burst into flames as it smacked into a wall on the right side of the grand central. Ty and Pop sped away onto the interboro into Bklyn.

Chapter 40

Firefighters and cops were using portable fire extinguishers to put out the blaze, once they had the fire in control and out they found DS and Daruis burnt remains. Wanda was in the kitchen (the car was in her name) putting the dishes in the dishwasher when the phone rang, Wanda was thinking this fucking phone just keeps ringing. Wanda puts down the plates and reaches for the phone, but by the time she got there it stopped ringing. As soon as she was about to walk away it started to ring again. Wanda" hello, how can I help you?" Wanda hears a unfamiliar voice" is this Mrs. Springs?" Wanda" yes it is, who is this?" the voice" detective Mason we need to see you ASAP, a car is on the way there to you now, I have some grave news for you, your husband and son was in a bad car wreck." Wanda dropped the phone and fell to her knees and grasped her hands tight. Wanda" please Lord, let this be a dream, not my baby. Det, Mason was yelling in the background " Mrs. Springs are you there, please a car is on the way!!" boom, boom the cops was knocking on Wanda's door, she was in a daze she didn't hear it until the eighth bang. She got up off the floor and let them in.

Chapter 41

Carlos, Gloria and R was sitting at the table with a brand new bottle of Hennessey, with three full cups. R said," I can't believe my dude DS was slipping like this, this isn't him." Gloria said," the baby" her eyes was swelling already form all the crying she had done, she grabbed her glass drank it and walked to the back. Los said," I can't stop thinking of my dude how could this have happened. I keep asking Wanda who the fuck he brought there, all she kept saying was us and their family. I am going to lay of her and let her clear her thoughts but we got to get to the bottom of this!!"

R said," I know who did it or had something to do with it and I am going to hit thun up something nice." Slipping on his drink. R says," Gloria is going to see Wanda now. She is at her mother's she doesn't even want to go back to the house". Gloria walked out the back with some bags in her hand and kissed R, then Los and walked out the door. Tank was awaiting her, he held the door open and they drove off. R said," we got to find a way to get at Pop, it had to be him or he knows something about it.

Lil Darius!!" R threw the glass against the wall and it shattered. All he could do was cover his face with his hands to cover his pain.

Chapter 42

Gloria was helping Wanda get dressed. Today was going to be one of the toughest days of her life, seeing her only son and husband laid to rest. Wanda had an all black dress on her belly was huge. She had a glow, you could see the radiance of her bringing new life into this world was there, but her eyes was full of sorrow and you could see the disconsolateness there. She was distraught, Gloria helped her get out of the chair and they walked out into the awaiting limo. There was a light drizzle in the air, the threat of thunderstorms were present.

Burner one of R's mans was with them, he stayed with them every since that happened to DS. They finally arrived at Quinn's funeral home on Broadway in Astoria. The parking lot was full, tons of people came out to pay respect to DS. The limo had an assigned spot across the street from the funeral home. Once they parked Burner got out, on-point looking around he noticed R parking his bike. R walked over and Wanda and Gloria got out of the limo. R hugged Wanda R" how are you mom" Wanda said, " I am holding up!" R said," you know I will take care of everything whatever you need just call me!" Wanda said," I know R, Darren loved you, L, Carlos and Shakim y'all were just like his brothers"

R said," a person isn't measured by their intentions. They're measured by their deeds and their actions alone. At the end of the day the proof is in the pudding." That statement made Wanda smile in light of the situation. DS always said that. She hugged R, he said," I loved DS and Darius so much I cant go in there and see them like that". Gloria hugged her man. A tear rolled down R's eyes, he walked off and told Burner to follow him. R got his self together wiped the tears from his eyes. R ordered," Burner hold them down, by all means I will be close by. You see them two Chevy' Tahoe's, that's the fucking police, Ms. Pat hit me and told me they was taking pictures of everybody coming in or out." smiling " You don't got no record and as many dudes as you mercked if they only knew" Burner laughed he never says too much he just always listened and if R told him to get somebody, you better believe their head was off. R said," you know I hate the pigs, plus I cant see my bro like that! I will be right here, don't let nothing happen to them. Fuck the pigs" before he could finish, Burner interrupted " I am going out blazing I got the black mac-10 with three clips and I never miss, I got this playboy." R never really questioned Burner's loyalty or the fact he gets busy but R always played mind games to have all of his soldiers on point. R knew that you don't go to war unprepared or under financed that's why we paid everyone around him well, R also knew a few things like the streets don't got no sympathy for nobody that's why he always enforced carrying the joint everywhere he went.

He is going to kill Pop it doesn't matter if Pop's grandmother or Jesus Christ him self was there he would still kill them all, no sympathy and he wouldn't be amped about it. It was just something that had to be done. A fucking walk in the park as far as he was concerned. He felt an obligation to DS and to lil Dee to make sure it gets done. His Gloria felt the same way R did and she was there to watch Wanda also, so R felt good about it. R walked and started his Honda CBR 1100 and took off. He pulled over to a group of ten bikes and parked, the rest of his crew were waiting for him. They were close enough to watch but far enough not to be seen. Once the service was done Bundy and agent Crowley was in back of the Tahoe taking photos of everyone that came out of the funeral home. Bundy pointed to Carlos and Tracey coming out, Bundy says, "that's Carlos Cordero aka Los!" telling agent Crowley.

Chapter 43

Wanda, Gloria, Burner, fat Shakim and Wanda's mother and father along with DS's mom sat in the front row. Miss Pat, Karen, Leroy and Carlos was kneeling before Darius's little casket, this was the first time in his life that he ever seen a casket that small. He felt hopelessness and homicidal at the same time. He felt terrible that he couldn't help DS and Darius, he was consumed with anger and rage at Pop for doing this. Carlos moved from lil Dee's casket and went to DS's. Carlos knelt over and kissed his brother on the cheek, said his praise in hope of acceptance of his brother and his son into the pearly gates of heaven. He got up and sat silently in the back row, and his girl Tracey came to join him. The service was a one-day thing, after the burial everyone came to the Jacob Riis Center to eat and to celebrate DS and Darius's life.

Carlos wasn't surprised to see how so many people came out to see his blood off. Everyone was around politicking, eating and reminiscing about their memories of DS. "He was a good dude, I am going to miss him, you know he brought me my first $1000 pair of gators for this party we was going too. Damn we had a blast, it was just me and thun word!" Tank was telling Tamia. DS was a quiet and strong dude, he was always humble but didn't take shorts from no one. Shakim was standing there talking to Mr. Gray.

Mr. Gray walked up to the stage in the center and grabbed the micro-phone," hello" tapping the mic gesturing for the director Mr. Alston to get the sound tighter. Mr. Alston was fumbling with the dials, once he got it right he put his thumb up. Mr. Gray said," good evening to everyone I am so sorry we are gathering here yet again for a senseless killing of two of our own. The whole room was playing close attention to every word that came out of Mr. Gray's mouth. This is too much for me. I seen Darren grow up since as long as I can remember, I am lost for words about lil Dee as we called him. I brought a guest speaker with me today to help me with this cause, please everybody here is preacher Ronald Holt" everyone gave him a loud applause.

Rev. Holt took the mic from Mr. Gray, Rev. Holt said, "thank you everyone, thank you David, my deepest apologies Mr. Gray." Mr. Gray and the crowd laughed Mr. Gray kneeled his head to Rev. Holt. Rev. Holt continued," I was deeply troubled when I got the phone call about Darren and this child. I shook cause this is a sensitive issue for me, it was sickening that this happened to this child. This is the clearest evidence that there is a war going on in the African-American community. This is a class conflict that pits brother against brother and neighbors against neighbors and because the enemy looks like us, walks like us it is easy to ignore the battle lines. This war has already claimed some of the brightest stars in our families and many of the future victims of this war will embody all of the hopes we have for the black race. I look at my 6 year old grandson and cringe knowing that unless the God- fearing and decent among us find a way to win this war one day, I will be sending him to the front lines against black children who for whatever reason have already lost their souls. Darius Smith was just a child an innocent soul, what makes a person or causes them to wantonly and blatantly hatch such an ill-conceived plan? To go and do something like this? What makes them do it? Rev. Holt broke down," I am shell shocked by what happened to the Smith family, we must take a stand". All the ladies, wives, and mothers broke down with Rev. Holt" this was a life that didn't have to be took, these young cats don't realize the value of life, it hurts my soul to even think that this type of violence is so woven into this culture that murder has become a symbol of manhood." Before he could finish R was standing in the corner with blood shot eyes looking at the Rev. Holt and walked out. Tank walked out behind him and opened the bottle of champagne he had, he tiled the bottle and poured half of it out. Tank said," to my thun DS"

Chapter 44

In the Bronx Pop, Pernell, Moon and a few dudes were standing on the corner of University Avenue and 225th. There were ten motorcycles lined up on the block, Pop threw the remains of his turkey and Swiss hero in the trashcan. Pop always rode bikes, he was a great rider, riding bikes was one of his main hobbies. Pop and his crew always rode them, when they were involved in some foul shit they are great escape tools for his line of work. Pop felt that if you're a criminal be on 24 hours a day and stick to your trade and sticking up was his, Pop loved to rob drug dealers most of the time he would get them in their homes very rarely he got drugs, because the smart ones never had them in there houses. But after he got the info from them regarding their stash houses, he would just take the drugs to Tree, who would then get them sold. Pop was waiting for Lucky to come meet him. A black livery car pulled up Lucky paid the driver, got out and walked over to Pop. Pop didn't really like Lucky, he never did when they was in prison, Pop never really went out of his way to politick with him. When Pop wasn't in the box, he walked around the 4 building freely. He would just say what's up to him in passing. Pop didn't like the fact, that Lucky was running around the spot telling everybody that they were peeps. Pop really didn't know thun like that. Pop knew Lucky was just using his name to keep dudes off him. Pop's rep was crazy in the clink, Pop always put in that knife and razor work. A lot of the gees respected him. His comrade Steel was running the house Lucky first went too, at the time Pop was in the box for a multiple stabbing. Steel asked Lucky where he was from, Lucky told him "QB" and the first names that came out his mouth was Pop's and Jewel's. Steel had a lot of juice in the spot, so Capt. Hynes took him to see Pop. Steel told Pop about Lucky, Pop couldn't really recall dude, but he told Steel to hold him down because he is from Pop's hood. Now don't get it twisted Lucky puts it in, but Pop didn't like that shit, his motto was stand on your own. Rep your hood but never over talk and Lucky was like that, an over talker. Pop knew this is how it goes, you might be telling a dude who had a beef with someone from your hood, that you and that person is cool that's your man and you rock with him not knowing they are rocking you to sleep, you are putting yourself in danger, the whole time you are running your mouth about whoever, you're in a house full of his enemies, now you got yourself in a jam in big trouble.

When Pop was in that situation he always said" he didn't know anybody and what's up?" In a threatening matter, Pop knew the game, he rocked a lot of dudes like that, he played that cool role deliberately to see in you are F or F (friend or foe) in any house or jail he was in. Lucky walked up to Pop and gave him a dap, Pop knew of Lucky's obvious motive for not liking L, but he was still trying to figure out why he hated R, DS, and Carlos like he did. Being that he was a life-long resident of QB and the opportunity was always present for him to move on them. Pop knew one of the reasons that Lucky was helping him was money, the root to all evil and the other he couldn't put his finger on. Pop knew there was no honor among thieves, its all about capitol gain. It was just business they had to do together, they had a common enemy and the alliance they had could never be fully trusted, but Pop knew one thing and after he puts the bullets in R and Carlos he was going to flip and bang Lucky's ass out too, he made sure that was on his agenda. It was just basic logic to Pop and for now he would just act collectively. He was aware of the power of coalitions and uniting against common enemies and him getting close to Carlos and them transcended everything else. Pop went to the bag on his bike and gave Lucky $15 grand. Lucky quickly stuffed it in his pocket. Pop said," what's good Lucky anything new for me?" Lucky said," everything is good, shit my pockets are a lot fatter. Smiling," I got the word that R and Carlos are going to the club in a few days" Pop didn't show the excitement in his eyes, Pop said," where at?" Lucky always had to rethink his words before he talked around Pop. Pop was sharp, on-point, an extremism, he lived by this rule, watch what you say, think before it's said, and mean what you say because once it's said there isn't no turning back from it. That's one of the main reasons why he didn't drink and smoke, he always felt that doing that clouds your judgment and thoughts. Lucky knew this about Pop. Lucky said," the same spot from last time, the one I was telling you about." Pop said, " ok I will be there' Lucky said," they're having a party there for Play, he just came home that's one of R's mans from the 40 side of tenth street. On the 26th, which is in three weeks, they'll be in the VIP section. Pop turned and walked back to his crew they all got on their bikes and took off.

Chapter 45

It's was a beautiful day, the sun was blazing the temperature was 95 degrees. R, Los, Tank, Burner, Boo, Play and the rest of the crew were having this big bang. It was Tank's birthday so they were celebrating. Tamia was on the grill flipping burgers, Gloria, Miss Pat, and Miss Isabelle was talking away, DJ Funky Child was playing the old school jams. Everything was going lovely, Camilla walked up, and she had a blacken and bruised left eye. Miss Pat got up from here chair and walked over to Camilla and hugged her. Miss Pat said, "are you alright sweetheart?" Camilla said," yes, I am okay Miss Pat!" Miss Pat was about to say something else but Miss Isabelle grabbed her hand, Miss Isabelle knew how Miss Pat felt about domestic violence. Miss Pat went and sat back down, she heard about Lucky beating Camilla up, everyone was talking about it and she felt sorry for her. Miss Pat seen it so many times on her 69 years on this earth, She guessed poverty brought some depression and some men couldn't handle it and took it out on their woman. She seen a dear and close friend of hers get abused and she despised it. Her friend Tammy fell for this ex junkie Dave, Miss Pat knew Dave wasn't right for Tammy, Miss Pat knew that Dave was going to use again, and she was right. Dave used all types of drugs but mostly crack cocaine he loved it. He started whipping Tammy's ass.

Miss Pat tried to get her to call the cops but she refused. Tammy would never say or do anything wrong about Dave, all she would say is that he loved her, even after he took all her pension money and smoked it up. Miss Pat tried telling her love wasn't like that, but Tammy wouldn't listen. Miss Pat helped her with the rent money that month but Tammy stayed with him. Miss Pat hated woman beaters. Camilla asked," Miss Isabelle is Carlos around?" Miss Isabelle pointed to where Carlos was talking to R. Camilla said," take care y'all, thank you Miss Isabelle!" then walked to where Carlos and R was talking. As she approached they stopped talking. R and Carlos simultaneously said' what's up Cam?" Camilla said," hey R, Carlos can I talk to you for a few?" R had a surprised look on his face, he was wondering what that bitch wanted. Carlos said," for sure what's up?" and he walked off with her. Camilla was once a bad broad, she just gained a lot of weight in these last few years, but you could still see the beauty in her face. Camilla said," Los how is everything going?" Carlos said," Good, I see you got into some type of fight" Carlos didn't know what happened to her. Camilla said, "that punk motherfucker Lucky" she started crying Carlos put his arm around her, he told her "calm down." Carlos walked her to the benches, they both sat down. Camilla breathing heavily, she sucked it in and blew out a big breath. Camilla" that son of a bitch Lucky came to my house all drunk and shit wanting to fuck me. I wasn't with it I told him to go back to wherever he came from and not to come over here with that mess, he knows I hate that shit. I tried to push him towards the door, he grabbed me by my hair and starting telling me that I am a chicken head bitch and that he was just using me to get info on y'all. I broke loose from his grip then pushed him, he stumbled against the wall. Then he went on saying that it was my fault DS and Darius was dead and shit like that. Carlos was stunned when he heard that, Camilla continued on "I was like what motherfucker? Lucky said you heard me right bitch you told me where DS lived and I told Pop and I got $ 15,000 gees for it. Matter of fact bitch give me that shirt I brought you, that you got on hoe!" Lucky advanced towards me and punched me in the eye, everything went kind of black, I fell down and he started kicking me a lot of times. I just covered up. Carlos was mad as hell. Camilla said," he was saying all types of shit then he ran out the door, that bitch ass nigger!" Carlos was listening intensely, "word and what else he say?" Camilla" that motherfucker is pussy, he's lucky he was in jail or he would have been murked.

He said Pop is going to kill all of y'all and that he is going to take over, he was just going on and on." Carlos said," thanks Cam, do you got somewhere to stay cause, he is going to realize that he shouldn't of told you some of that shit and really think about it what if Pop finds out. Camilla thought of all of these things before she got the courage to tell Carlos, she had a secret crush on him for years. She felt he was the only one she could trust. Camilla said," yeah I am out of here going to my aunt's crib in D.C. I could never face Wanda again in life, knowing that some shit I said got lil Dee, she stopped then said" I can't believe it." Carlos held her," calm down Cam. Here take this $500 go get you're shit and go to a hotel until your ready to go." Carlos reached in his pocket and gave her 20 $20 dollar bills. Carlos said," give me a pen so I can give you my number and you call me when you're at the hotel" Camilla went in her bag and gave him a pen, he wrote the number down. Carlos said, "go ahead and make sure u call me". Camilla said, "thank you Los!" Carlos said," nah thanks for hollering at me".

Carlos was steaming and furious inside, he just sat there and watched Camilla as she walked out the park.

Chapter 46

On Blake and rockaway Carlos, R and Tank was sitting in Tank's Green Chevy blazer. Carlos broke the long silence with a shout" we got to get this dude Pop and whoever's with him. R was starring out the window his mind was in another place, when Los spoke out he was brought back. Tank said," hell yeah, everybody!!" You could sense the change in Tank since this whole thing started with Pop. Tank was always ready, he always had the hammer on him. R was on all of them about that. Telling him just be prepared, always on point, to be the aggressor. R studied the art of war, As a Man thinketh, the laws of power and all of them books, he knew them all by heart, back and forth and he implied them in his plan from the jump. He knew he was going to rock Head and whoever else was in his way. R started plotting as soon as he heard of Head's weak ways. Head was strong when he was younger but he lost his way. R knew Head was losing his strength and R was just getting stronger. This shit with Pop was way out of hand, he knew they had to end this fast before anymore of his people got hurt. Ant-wop and Prinz walked up to the car R got out and went to meet them. R said," what's up?" Wop and Pee" what's up?" they exchanged greetings and R said," I need y'all to handle something for me!"

Chapter 47

Lucky was in the courtyard on the 41 side of Vernon blvd talking to T-gee. Lucky had this blue and orange Met's jacket on, a pair of blue jeans and a pair of orange and blue Nike sneakers. He also had on this big gold cross-filled with diamonds, he just brought from the diamond spot on 47th street. He was standing in an ill stance detailing how Cee was standing in the club the other night. T-gee just started laughing. T-gee said, 'word Cee was showing his ass last night huh?" Lucky said,' word is bond that nigga had us all laughing. We was in a mini cipher, this dude Cee was dipping down low doing all the old school dances, we was cheering him on, the club was alright last night God word!!" T-gee said, "damn I missed a good night, yeah nigga you still pussy-whipped over Cam?" Changing the subject, Lucky said, " come on God, u know I don't get p-whipped, I get the bitches dick-whipped, I turn them out!!" T-gee started laughing, T-gee said," yeah okay God but I heard different." Lucky said," I mean hey, she did have a fat pussy but I wasn't whipped, I whipped her ass!" T-gee said, " you are a crazy dude and gives Lucky a pound. T-gee said," yo God I got to bounce, got to go to work in the am." Lucky said," u still got that punk ass job?" T-gee said," yeah bad enough you got me out here to 3 in the morning and I got to be there at 8, shit I am outta here!!" They shook hands and T-gee walked towards his building.

Lucky started walking to 41st-Road and 10th street. He parked his dark grey Toyota Camry back there. As he walks to the car, he notices one of his tires are flat. Lucky curses loudly," shit what the fuck!" he kneels down to check on it. Lucky says," fuck" he stands and puts his keys in the passenger door, he didn't notice Wop and Pee jump out the van parked directly right across from him. Wop put the 9mm to Lucky 's head. Wop says," don't fucking move" Pee got his pistol on Lucky's back, Prinz searched him and took his small 22 out of Lucky's waist. Lucky says," take the chain man just don't kill me" trying to talk his way out of this jam he was in. Ant-Wop laughs, says," nigger I don't want your motherfucking chain" Pee snatches the chain off of Lucky's neck. Pee says," but I want that bad ass shit!" Lucky tried to move for it he knew this wasn't no regular stick up, but Wop and Pee was all over him pistol-whipping him savagely, they started dragging him into the park, there was a small park on 41 road with handball courts in it. They took Luckys unconscious body behind the handball courts and put two in his head.

Chapter 48

The older Spanish woman Maria was working for the parks dept. she was headed behind the handball court to clean up, once she was back there she smelled this horrible stench. She saw an odd pile of leaves, she went to put them in her big black garage bag, she noticed the stench was getting stronger, being nosy like she always is she move the leaves with the rake she had in her hand" Oh my God!!!' she screamed and took of running back to her co-workers. Yelling" someone call the police" her district manager walked to her "what's wrong?" she just pointed to the back he wanted to go check it out before he called the cops. He saw a lot in his days, it was most likely a dead dog or cat or something. He went back there, he seen a stark-naked male body with two holes in his head.

The whole block was taped off it was a big crowd gathering to see what was going on. Det. Bundy and his partner Franco arrived on the scene, they flashed their badges to the uniforms by the yellow police tape. They walked back to the crime scene, the two CSI cops were kneeling over Luckys body, the Chinese CSI cop, officer Wong said, "hey Det. Bundy and Franco' they both greeted him back. Wong says," they did a job on this one, who ever did this cut his balls off!" Bundy says," wow for Christ sake, the monkeys in the poor-jects are going a little crazier now huh?" Officer Wong didn't really care for Bundy's racial epithets he was always yelling. Officer Wong" yes it is bad, his genitals were out there by the hand ball court like some sick joke!!" Franco walked to where the other sheets was and lifted it up. Franco "unfucking believable.' Bundy asked," any suspects? Did anyone see anything!!"Yelling towards the crowd.

Wong says," we had a few calls but nothing solid to go on. Bundy turns to his partner" lets go Franco, and shake the fucking trees to see what comes out!!" Franco" lets go!!' He was more than ready he hated niggers and spics " lets go hunting in the concrete jungle and coerce the coons to tell" Laughing he patted Bundy on his back as they walked to their car.

Chapter 49

R, Wop and Pee were sitting on the stoop of the brownstone R just brought. Wop says, "we keep checking that crib for Pop, he is never there, this fucking dude is like a fucking ghost, we been checking all of his known hang outs, we can't get at this dude, what is he hiding under a fucking rock or something?" laughing R said," yo, we are going to run into him sooner or later I just don't want dudes getting off point. You know everything thun set out to do he done it successfully so you know we got to stay light footed and ready." A man who doesn't think and plan ahead will find trouble right at his door, shit I learned that from the thing with DS, can't let this dude catch us slipping." Prinz says, "oh for sure that's real, we are on our toes, we are trying to hunt this dude down, he don't know us so we got a little advance on dude. R you know how it is you told us to hit that dude and we were on it It'll be a minute but we will get this Pop dude too." R says," without a doubt my dude" and they walked in the house.

Chapter 50

Carlos, Tank and R were freshly-dipped and ready to go the Vixen bar, the club they booked up for Play's coming home party. Carlos had on a new pair of Gucci sneakers, beige pair of polo shorts and a black polo shirt. R had on a sky blue fila suit with the sneakers paired to match, R always wore shorts under his sweat pants to keep the glock intact. Tank was wearing a red and white adidas suit with red and white shell toes. They walked out the block of 10th street to 40 ave and 12th street. Carlos and Tank got in Carlos's black Cadillac STS. R walked to his Honda CBR 1100. It was a cool breeze blowing and the stars were out. Carlos hoped for the best and was prepared for the worst everyday he stepped out the house and today was no different. The paper was rolling in, everything was good but he still felt fucked up he lost a lot to the game. Richie, Ebony, Darren, DS, Darius one of his best friends L to 20 years in prison. He knew the reality of things right now so all he could do was deal with it. He knew that some people see more in a walk around the block, then others see in a trip around the world. Shit in these past years Carlos seen and been thru a lot. Tank taps Los's "shoulder you ready?" Carlos said," 4sure lets go. Carlos pulls off, R and Wop right behind him. They're racing across the bridge, Carlos is flooring it, tank grabbed his seat belt, Tank said," come on, now how come every time we go anywhere you and this sick dude have to race?" Carlos, I got this dude!" and flies by R and Wop. Carlos is hitting 87, Tank grasping the door panel and the arm-rest. Tank says," come on thun, you know I hate this shit!!" Looking nervously out the front window. Carlos says, "all right kid chill!" They cruise the rest of the way there. Carlos and Tank drives pass the Vixen bar to see if they can park in the front. It is crazy crowed out there. Pop, Rah and Tooter are standing in the crowd, hiding in the crowded line behind the chicks they brought will them. They see Tank's car drive by and Play's new Benz. Carlos pulls up to Barkim the head of security in the spot. Carlos said," what's up kid?" Barkim walks up to the car "what's good Los, here's a parking pass, go park and walk up to the front of the line.' R and Wop are just riding slowly around the block. Tank pulls in the parking lot right around the corner, Play, R and Wop follow. Tank gives the parking attendant the pass so they don't have to pay. Tank tells the attendant to park both cars on the top level and gives him two hundred dollar bills. R and Wop pull over there bikes, R said," yo what the fucks up with Bar? I am not feeling this parking in the lot, we gave them $15,000 for this fucking party why we got to park in this fucking lot?" Carlos says," he (Bar) was like to tell Black and Shakim to move their cars and we park there, but I wasn't going to call them and tell they to move they're already in the spot, so I told him fuck it thun we're good, we aren't going to stay long anyway and he gave us parking passes. Anyway we are right in the front, lets just get mad bottles and blow out." R displaying his nastiest scowl said" I am parking my bike in the fucking front, fuck all that other shit" R put his helmet back on and peeled off. As R is riding back around to the club, he sees this chick Pearl he use to fuck with. In R's mind" damn I loved and miss that pussy.' R pulls up on her beeping his horn, her fine ass just keeps on walking. Her girlfriend Tina the jump off said," I think he is beeping at us girl!!!" Pearl looks as they're walking says" fuck them" R pulls up his helmet and drives right on the side of her then says" damn its like that now butter!!" Pearl stops when he said butter only one man called her that, she knew it was R. R pulls over, and Wop pulls on the side of him. Pearl runs up hugs him. Pearl said," oh shit butter what's good?" R hugs her and feels her fat ass, he is thinking of the ways he use to fuck her, damn he is missing it!! R said," Pearl what good butter?" Pearl said, "damn I really miss u baby!!" R said," word I miss u too!" R and Pearl are holding each close and they continue to talk. Carlos, Play and Tank are walking up the block, they see Justice and a few other dudes from the hood are there and Carlos isn't really playing attention. Pop and Ra are looking, Tooter is trying to get at all the chicks that walk by or that are on the line. Pop pulls out two 45's Rah follows his lead and pulls out too, Tooter sees this and grabs this chick, then yells at her move!!

Carlos is looking at the line and sees that there is something going on. He sees Pop come out the crowd with two guns raised. First he let off one shot and everybody was running, then three more bam, bam, bam! One of the shots grazed Carlos's arm, he got low, pulled out and starting shooting, he took off running towards the parked cars. Tank pulled out and starting firing at Pop, Ra and Tooter. Tank fired twice striking Ra in the shoulder and the right leg, Ra fell to the pavement, but heart is never a substitute for brains. Tank started running towards the falling Ra, seeing his comrade down Pop sends four at the oncoming Tank, which hits him four times, two in the stomach, the chest and knee. Tank hits the cement sidewalk hard. Los is behind the parked cars in front of the club, he reloads and starts blazing at Pop and Tooter. Pop runs towards this group of girls that are so much in shock they didn't take off running like the rest of the crowd, Pop tucks one of his 45's in his waist and takes hold of one of the girls, he puts her in a choke hold, she is yelling at the top of her lungs. The eruption of gunfire and the crowd breaking up, came to the attention of R, he pushes Pearl off him and starts riding towards the sounds of gunfire. R and Wop sees two dudes on the floor, Pop in the middle of the street holding some lady with a gun to her head and some other guy standing beside Pop. R and Wop start letting it go at Pop, Carlos starts firing at Pop and Tooter, between the both of them, Pop doesn't got much of a choice he lets the girl go so he can get his other weapon. The girl tried to run but got hit in the buttocks and back. Pop and Tooter are firing at both Carlos and R but to no avail. One of the bullets hit Pop in the back of his head, he falls sideways. Tooter runs in the direction of the club entrance, Carlos hits him in his neck, Tooter's legs give out on him. Carlos ran over to him and finished the job, three in his face.

The sirens from the approaching cop cars were blaring. At the entrance of the club two off duty cops bust out the door, displaying their shield's, ordering Carlos to drop the gun. Several police cruisers are turning the corner behind R and Wop. R and Wop take off down the block. Wop is following R's every move. R gets to the corner and sees another cop cruiser so he gets on the sidewalk and goes back towards the way he just came. Flying pass the oncoming cop cars, once he hits the corner he breaks right onto traffic, weaving his way thru, the car's horns were incessantly beeping, R and Wop went right, then left then out of sight. R knew in his heart it was better to kill or die then to surrender or live the rest of his life in prison. No way was he going back to jail, not with a third strike for life, that much was settled in his mind. So he knew he was willing to do anything for that not to happen. Carlos took immediate action, he took off towards the corner, wishing he could make it to his car, as he turned the corner this one cop smashed him over the head with his night stick, sending him crashing to the pavement, again the flash and pain. The nightstick bounced off his skull, blood ran down into his eyes, a forearm went around his throat in a chokehold, he saw the legs in blue uniform pants. One cop stepped on his head and grounded his face into the pavement. Then they violently dragged him away he was manacled from behind and thrown in the rear of a police cruiser.

Chapter 51

EPILOGUE

Carlos's cell cracks open, he walks out to see Miss Jackson this female co, she says" mail time.!" She yells out," Smith" this dark skinned dude walks up to her. She asks him his id numbers, he say" 8668" she hands him two letters, he walks off and this process continues. Finally she screams out "Cordero!" does he walk to the front he always stood in the back looking at all those around him. He always laughed to his self because some of the convicts get upset for not receiving any mail but constantly stand in the front at mail call everyday, then he thought to his self maybe that's the only hope they have of someone caring enough for them to drop a simple letter in the mail. Carlos walked up to C.O. Jackson she was a good-looking sister he thought as he got the letters from her and went back to his cell. He received three letters, he opened the one from his girl Tracey, she always sprayed his favorite perfume on every letter she sent him, he laughed at some of the things she wrote him and smiled. Then he opened the letter from his mother, she always wrote and asked about his well-being, he told her not to write so much that he was ok, but she always sent him 8 or 9 letters a week. She didn't like the fact that he was in there. He knew he no ones parent or love ones wanted that for their people but it was part of the game he was in, so he abided by the rules, no snitching and stand like a man in any situation. Some dudes are unloyal motherfuckers and they will tell on their mothers to get out. You don't tell on your comrades when you live the same life as them. You live the way you chose and abide by that. They can't bend nor break him only the strong survive. The last letter was from his boy Shakim, opening the letter he took out the pictures he sent and five hundred dollar bills slipped out. The photos were of his boy fat Sha was with these two fine chicks with fat asses, Carlos was like "okay my boy is doing it!" the second flick was of Richie, DS, Wanda, Ebony, Darren R, Shakim and himself, when they were younger on the block.

Carlos starts to read the *letter Peace and Love: big brother how are you holding up? I am in hopes that you are mentally strong and holding on. I will be back up to New York your next court date. I am going to stay with your moms and Tracey. your moms is doing well I just got off the phone with her before I started writing this letter. She is worried sick about you and Jewel's. y'all are in all of prays. The last time I was up there. I put new flowers on DS. Richie and lil Dee's grave. I miss all of the crew so bad* (tears rolled down Carlos's cheek onto the paper, he wiped his eyes and continued reading) *if it wasn't for y'all I never would of make it out of there. I owe y'all everything for the man I am today. All of the monetary things and the life lessons y'all gave me are priceless couldn't learn that in any school I attended, and I will try to apply those lessons in all I do in my life. I will always be there for y'all as long as God permits me to have air in my lungs. I love it here in ATL, my new job is great, six figures now*☺ *I met this new lady friend Marilyn, that's the one in the flick with me and her sister, she is the one on the right. She is coming up with me to see you, you know I need your approval. Not serious yet, but its looking good. I been hearing the same shit is going on in the projects, but it will never be the same with y'all gone. No need for me go there. Anyway later for that bullshit. Yo, I was at the hot strip club Magic city and ole boy walked in, I was so happy to see him.* (Carlos smiled he knew who Shakim was referring to) *that's my dude, he is still the same, in good health. G was with him too*☺ (Carlos thought shit he knew that, R will never leave Gloria's side and neither will she leave him) *yeah, I am flying moms, Tracey, Wanda and her little girl the whole family down for thanksgiving, shit you will have tons of flicks from that☺ I will be to see you before the next court date. Love you my big brother!! Peace: Shakim*

On the count, C.O. Brock yelled, that brought Carlos back to his current situation, he put the letter on the bed and went to look out of his cell window.

An Excerpt from Adele's flowers Available This Fall.

Jennifer was at her desk looking over her paperwork for her upcoming case. She had to be in court in a few hours to get the deed, the terms and conditions of the Lexington building. That's the property they are working on. Her phone rang, an eerie sense of foreboding hung in the air. She sensed something was wrong, she picked it up on the fifth ring. " Hello", the female voice said on the other line. Immediately she knew it was Sarah's voice. Jennifer, hello Sarah. Sarah, I got some terrible news for you, Miss Adele passed away! Jennifer's eyes still wide with disbelief. She quickly dismissed Sarah's statement. Jennifer, what are you saying, what are you talking about? breathing heavily. Pain, fear and fury all mingled into one. Miss Adele had an enormous presence in her life, if it wasn't for her she would have never made it out of her past life. Miss Adele showed her and taught her so much. She rolled a pencil between her thumb and forefinger and remembered back to the time when she grew up. Jennifer grew up in Queens, New York in public housing. Although Queens has the least number of public housing developments at 28 compared to Brooklyn's 101 developments it still took its toll on the youth living there. Ravenswood Houses where she grew up at consists of 31 buildings, six stories tall, an estimated 4,541 people live there. Col. George Gibbs, a businessman who developed the complex acquired the land in 1814. In 1848 there were several mansions built on this land, but the high-class housing did not survive. In 1875 the first residential buildings were erected and the mansions were converted into offices and boarding houses. In the beginning stages of the development the entire housing complex consisted of Caucasians of middle income, but the Government started replacing most of these tenants with African American and Latino families. This policy provided safe and sanitary housing to many low income African American and Latino families. However it also resulted in racially motivated conflicts between their children. Jennifer could never forget all of the teasing she received from her being biracial. Jennifer Rivers mother was white and her father Cherokee Indian and black. Her mother's name was Lorna Rivers. Lorna moved to New York City at the age of 19 years old looking for a better life, she was from a small town in Portland, Oregon. Her father Jason Taylor was a hard working man a cement laborer, he was a union man, local 76. Lorna and his relationship was wonderful in the beginning, but after an injury at work and couldn't work anymore, he turned into a different person. He started drinking heavily and got hooked on the painkillers that were giving to him to help ease the pain of his right hand that was broken by a gyratory crusher. Lorna was able to secure a position with a bank and this made her happy because she wanted to contribute to the well being of her family and with her husband being out of work she was not able to. As the weeks went by Jason kept showing up at her job demanding money. He became deeply depressed and more dependent on Opioid a highly addicted morphine based drug, which the doctors stop prescribing to him. That's when the real problems began for them. By him constantly coming up to her job and disrupting her work, he got her fired. In between his drinking he would go out looking for work so he said. Still in all his hand was so badly damaged that he couldn't grasp and hold things like he used too. Thus limiting the type of work he used to get. This was a drastic change for the young couple with their little girl Jennifer there to provide for. With both of them without a steady job, Lorna went to the welfare office, it was hard for her to do, because she believed in working, but with Jason's current state and no money coming in, she had very little choice. Jason went to the unemployment office, there he ran into an old buddy of his Bowen. Bowen, what's up partner? Jason, trying to hold on! Bowen, I heard about your hand, did you contact the insurance agent about that? Jason, of course I did but that asshole foreman Samuel Rosen told them it was my fault, I tried to protest it to no avail.

ORDER FORM

40BEES ENTERTAINMENT, INC.
40-15 30TH AVENUE BOX 118
ASTORIA NY 11103
347-614-7967
WWW.40BEES.COM

TITLE: Looking Out My Project's Window........................$ 14.95
SALES TAX..$ 1.25
Shipping and Handling...$ 4.20
TOTAL: ....$ 20.40

PURCHASER INFORMATION

NAME:____
ADDRESS:______________________________________
CITY:________________ STATE:______ ZIP:________

40 BEES ENTERTAINMENT WILL DEDUCT 25% OFF THE SALE PRICE FOR ORDERS SHIPPED DIRECTLY TO CORRECTIONAL FACILITIES.

LOOKING OUT MY PROJECT'S WINDOW.................................$11.21
SALES TAX...$ .78
SHIPPING AND HANDLING...$ 3.20
TOTAL...$15.19